I0638212

Darren Francis was born in London but currently lives in leafy Bucks, writing and nurturing eschatological escape-plans.

His work has been published in a number of anthologies and journals, including Skin, emthree, Technopagan, britpulp! (print) and Retort, Why Vandalism?, Pulp, Catalyzer, ken*again, Sick Among The Pure, Starving Arts and Poetic Inhalation (online).

For further information and latest DF news go to
www.darrenfrancis.co.uk

Spell

Darren Francis

First published in 2008 by Public House Press

© Copyright Darren Francis 2007

Cover design by Darren Francis
Layout by Clai Philpott
Front cover Illustration by Darren Francis
Author photograph by Clai Philpott

ISBN 978-0-9556840-0-5

http://www.publichousepress.co.uk

http://www.darrenfrancis.co.uk

For Clai

Acknowledgements

Some of this material has previously been published, in different form, as follows: Binary in the July 2001 anthology emthree; Circulating under the title Circles in the January 2006 edition of Pulp; Disappear Here as part of Jeremy Deller's 1996 exhibition The Uses Of Literacy. Portions of Despite Straight Lines were published under the following titles and locations - Tatter in Sick Among The Pure (August 2004), Still Dead in Starving Arts (June 2004), Instead Of Stressed I Lie Here Charmed in Sick Among The Pure (October 2004), If God Were A Goth in Sick Among The Pure (June 2004).

DF thanks the following for their support, assistance and advice with his writing over the years: Judith Amanthis, Bennets, Catalyzer, Robyn Conway, Steve Coulson, Jeremy Deller, EditRed community, Eldo, em, Su Francis, Vivien Francis, Stephen Grasso, Colin Ireson, Jenn, Phil Jones, Ken*Again, Michael Kowalski, Simon Lewis, Mercy Manic, Elaine Palmer, Jac Palmer, Philpotts, Poetic Inhalation, Pulp Faction / pulp.net, Retort, Sick Among The Pure, Starving Arts, Tony White, Why Vandalism?

Contents

Despite Straight Lines

1.

Suzanne comes over to my flat to collect some things she left behind. Books, CDs, tee-shirts which I'd neatly folded and piled, a silk scarf from Thailand, a spider plant I keep forgetting to water.

She doesn't resemble herself; the first thing I think when Suzanne walks through the doorway. Her face a mock-up, not the face of the Suzanne in my memory, as If an actress had been hired to play her for me from here on in.

I busy myself in the kitchen making coffee, don't much fancy watching as she packs away her belongings. When I return to her she's kneeling on rust-coloured carpet, smiles up at me as she scans a CD inlay. Whoever this actress is, she's good; though her hair is cropped shorter, her mascara eagerly-applied, she's captured Suzanne's voice and mannerisms perfectly. She even wears the same clothes, the same dewberry scent, the same opaque heels, the same silver torc bracelet.

'Is this Tricky album yours or mine?' she says. 'I thought it was yours.'

'It's yours. I bought it for you.'

'Did you? I don't remember that.'

'Your birthday. That's why I put it in your pile of things.'

'But you like it too. You should have it.'

'I bought it again.'

She slides the CD into her bag. Reaches for a cigarette (blue box, I note - the Suzanne-hoaxer has got the wrong brand), realises she doesn't want one, returns the pack to her pocket, sips her coffee.

'I ought to go,' she says. 'I can't much stand being here. It feels too fresh.'

We stand face to face. Hold, rub noses like we used to. Then she leaves. Coffee-cup half-drained, cigarette stubbed, brown and sodden in the saucer.

I lose myself for a second. Adrift in wood-grain and beer-spills, the texture of slapdash paint-work. I click, switch out. I'm not here for a bit. Then I'm back. Where is now?

I'm sitting at my desk. Legs folded in an affected half-lotus. Eyes weighted, heavy-lidded, incipient dawn eroding circadian rhythms. Should go to bed, need to get up for work tomorrow. And I will, just not now. I have this moment to contend with first.

The TV is on, a mute dead-channel fuzz that lights half the room. David Bowie purls songs of astronomical love against clipped acoustic guitar. I see skies of rain. Swill Coca Cola. Can there be anybody in the western world who hasn't tasted Coca Cola? There's a magazine open in my lap. Why do women in bikinis tell me which hi-fi to buy? What business is it of theirs? Regardless of them the room's a mess once more, cups and plates and beer cans and clothes forming a second carpet. I can feel my blood cool as it runs out across my skin, as it beads, as it mats with hair. Remember the rhythmic slashes I made against my right forearm. Eight bassy cuts, a four four thrum. I watch the blood darken as it dries. It's as if, by staring long enough, I can see it changing colour, from keen crimson to sluggish platelet black.

'I still love you,' Suzanne had said, 'but I don't fancy you any more. It isn't fair to carry on being on with you. It isn't fair on you.'

How was I expected to cope artfully with that information? What could I do, how else could I deal with it, but to sleep with as many people as possible in order to make me feel like a viable commodity again? What would you have done?

Here's Matilda, Belgian beer in hand, chatting to Jess. Matilda clad in recent fashions, severe bob of her hair, logo tee-shirts wrapping her slight breasts. She scrys in beer fluff for future lottery numbers. Jess, male fag-hag, could never sleep with another man but finds the gay scene so fascinating. As usual we're in a bar, the kind of place with dance floor too, that doubles as a club. Or rather, they'll open up a back room, bring in a DJ and charge you to get in.

'If I really did that would you come after me?' Jess says. 'I mean, really? Honestly?'

'What do you think?' Matilda says. 'I mean, really? Honestly?'

'What the hell are you two on about?' I say.

Then a voice which is somebody's and 'oh' I say, and then a laugh, mine or theirs, whoever, chopped up in lighter-click and bass frequencies. 'Matilda hi,' I say. 'You're drunk,' she says, 'you're just after a shag,' she says. 'What do you fucking expect,' I say, 'after all that's happened and all,' I say. 'Oh fuck yeah, I guess, respect,' she says. And I say and she says and I say and she says then Jess comes back. 'She didn't give a shit,' he says. 'For me, for then, ahh fuck and there I was.' I think that's what he said, assume it relates to the sun-skinned and dreaded woman he was cruising earlier. The music is so loud I don't know what to think. We laugh, let the strobes absorb us.

I go to the toilet, stand pissing and gaze at myself in the mirror. Faintly bemused at what time and alcohol and depression have done to me - body lean but nearing that thirty-something beer swagger, face redefined by sweat, arms ravaged and scabby and slender as sleep. Don't quite feel drunk enough to dance but know I will soon. I don't drink to forget, I drink to remember. To flick switches, re-circuit channels. Cutting is similar, in a way, but my relationship with cutting is different; more refined, a gift to myself. Later. This isn't the time to be thinking about cutting.

Tonight's game is Shell. The name her parents gave her, the song they crooned as she swooned baby-null in their arms. 'Hi,' she says, and I 'hi' back. Or, I guess that's what she said. The smile that accompanied her words said 'hi', at least. We holler in each other's ears a while. Oakwood hair. Skirt adorned with cavorting flowers. Cigarette weaving like a wil-o-the-wisp. The dance-floor beats one

14

lovesong or another. I glimpse Matilda by the bar, leaning head to head with an owl-faced man; she flicks back her hair as he presses his mouth to her ear. Shell finishes her drink in two rapid gulps, bangs down the glass and I buy her another, and that's when we exchange names. On the dance floor we shimmy a while. My mind greased with alcohol, each movement so fluid, so seamless. I don't want sex with her, really, just want to wake up with her hands close, with that hair dashed across my pillows.

'What happened to your friends?' she says, 'I noticed you earlier, you were with a couple of people.'

'They're around. Jess was waiting for his dealer to turn up, I think.'

'Were you waiting for that, too?'

'No, not really.' Matilda gives owl-man the finger.

'So they won't mind if I borrow you for a while, then? I'm done with this place for tonight, anyway. What about you? Do you want to go somewhere else?'

As we leave the bar Shell checks her mobile for messages; none. Was she expecting somebody who didn't show? She slides the phone back in her pocket and I see her at last, in the crudity of neon as opposed to bar-light and beer-light. She's cute and I want her and my ears are ringing. A seed of sweat hugs her left eyebrow. Allusion to a double chin; give her a year or two. She hasn't mentioned my scabs yet, though it's hard to believe she's not noticed them; I'm wearing a short-sleeved tee-shirt. But people don't say anything, I've noticed, even when it's clear they've realised exactly what I've been doing.

'What sign are you?' she says.

'Sign?'

'Star sign. Get with the programme. You're a Scorpio, I know you are.' She smiles then, mischievous, lips out-turned and henna-coloured.

'Cancer,' I say.

'Both water signs. That figures.'

We taxi to her Cheapside flat. A cat greets us at the door, Bible-black with nose and paws of cream. She scoots it to the kitchen. Some milk and biscuits will keep it out of our way. And we kiss then. Shell's body pressed against me, her fingers closing so keen around my shoulder-blades. I whirl for the flushed curve of her cheeks, the just frankness of her mouth. She breaks the kiss, says 'this way', and I'm startled by the softness of her voice now, laugh at this and she takes it as a good sign, leads me to a bedroom that smells of lavender. Face in shade as she tugs her skirt off, hands behind her back and unclipping her bra. Breasts buoyant, nipples off-centre.

'I couldn't decide whether to go home with you or not,' she says. 'I was watching you for a while. You looked like you were having a good time. My friend didn't show up and I was so mad at him but I was curious, couldn't decide whether I should phone Ed and moan at him - Ed's the friend - or whether I should take you home with me, instead. I thought you were a bit strange.'

'You changed your mind, though.' What does it mean, when I chew my fingernails? What need is being served there? 'I'm glad you changed your mind.'

'Sure I changed my mind. Are you going to take your clothes off? I feel a bit self-conscious, standing here half-naked.'

Shell's fingers trace my arms as she undresses me, sometimes stray over my scabs and scars in an absent kind of way. She knows how I got them. Knows what I do, what I am; a cutter. But she doesn't mention it. Her sex-style so to-the-point, as if she'd learned from fashion magazines, had studied long and was only now applying the knowledge. 'Good,' she murmurs, her fingers dipping over my thighs, pulling me onto her. The first time I slept with somebody other than Suzanne was strange. It felt as if I were betraying her. I wanted to sleep with them because they weren't Suzanne; to see if I could, to see if the desire was still there, to see if I could remember. I guess I like Shell, but I couldn't objectively say. It's difficult to find fault in a person when you're about to come inside them.

Suzanne wasn't a cutter. How much of an impact did that have on us?

I only cut twice when we were together. She knows about the first; midsummer, so hot I could barely speak, we'd rowed about nothing but were both so drunk that everything was exaggerated, I lobbed a pint glass against a wall then ran the shards down my legs. 'Stupid, stupid, stupid,' she later said, bathing the cuts with a watery antiseptic. 'I know you've done this before but I'll never understand it. It makes no sense to me. I can't see why someone would want to do that to themselves.'

'Of course you don't understand it,' I told her. 'You don't do it. The only way anybody can understand it is if they need to do it,' but by then I was on her side in finding it a dumb thing, too.

'But why on earth would I want to?' she said. 'Why would anyone want to? I just can't see it. Do you mean that if I tried it, I'd see it? Because I just don't want to.'

17

'No, I don't mean that. It doesn't work like that, anyway.'

She doesn't know about the second occasion. A Christmas, she away at her sister's for a handful of days, me at home alone, a beer or few and Peter Gabriel on the stereo. I'd had one of those evenings when it seemed that all my deeds were denied, that I couldn't recognise the world that lurked beyond the door, that time existed only to strip me away. Those sorts of evenings. And the solution I hit upon, best means of making good, was by befriending my blades again. I wore long sleeves for a week to hide my healing.

Suzanne had known other cutters. Exes she'd mapped out for me, their mental and emotional topography such familiar territory. If she'd loved them, she could love me. But no.

When Shell and I are done with our rutting, I lay staring at the ceiling for a while. Dirty cream paint, squashed insects, a future I cannot comprehend. I curl myself around Shell instead.

'You're not a very happy person, are you?' she says.

'What makes you say that?'

'Am I wrong?'

'It's a long story.'

'I'm all ears.'

'How long have you got?'

'All the time in the world. As long as it takes.'

I peer about the room, the scarce objects that backcloth Shell's days. Wide bed with crimson sheets, dolphin postcards cheaply framed, crumpled clothes on hangers or floor, stacks of astrology paperbacks with water-warped covers. Could I open out here?

Solitary potted cactus. Lines of shoes leading to the door. It's nothing personal, I think, as I look at Shell; I wanted to get laid and you were there. Needed some closeness, the smell and sense of skin. But that's hard to voice without offending, so I nuzzle into her armpit and dream of sleep. Her back to me as I wrap around her, one hand at her belly and feeling each breath as it enters and escapes her. I used to believe that old adage about how love kills the demon, and that it was just a case of me finding the right person before all things resolved themselves. Now, I don't know if love kills the demon or not. Maybe all it can do is placate the demon. Or maybe not love; touch, contact, hugging. Empathy.

2.

Streets gush with rivers of rain. Nuclear trains rumble through the night. All is well. I sing for dead lovers, cleave woundings into my arm. Never alone, I surrender my hands, glory at the blood that runs down to pool at my palm, over life-lines and between fingers. Switch out. Resume reading my email.

'You don't feel real?' Jill, a one-week stand, retorted. Heft-limbed, neatest of faces. 'What could be more real than sex? Two bodies together? And working? And friends? Watching telly? Moaning about how crappy telly usually is? Going for a drink? Getting lost in music? What more do you need than that?'

'What more do I need? How long have you got?'

'Forget how long I've got. What do you see when you close your eyes?'

I met Louisa at a Nick Cave gig, and we lived together for three months. She was the first other cutter I knew. Angora and fake animal prints. Swallow tattoo on her left shoulder-blade.

'I am a kitten,' she said.

'A sex kitten?'

'No, just a kitten.'

Louisa had money. I sat alone watching the walls, her room scented with lemongrass, waited for her to come back from work. Picked my nails and smoked my cigarettes, stared with disregard at my body.

Our sex was violent. She'd prod and push me into whatever shapes and positions occurred to her, whichever best gave her game. My fingers tracing the whorl of her pubis, the tuck of her navel, the scimitars of her lips. She so arrogant when aroused, but I don't think Louisa liked sex that much. She knew its possibilities, that it was or could be the perfect analogue of love, that whatever one held onto and approximated as love could be replicated as sex. Good or bad. Cloying or casual or tight as catgut, intoxicated or indifferent. My body there, and hers too, she utterly shaven and smooth with sweat and freckles.

For Louisa, it was a thing to be used. An affirmation that she was different. If she cut, she wanted people to know about it. Gone midnight once, she screaming 'take all of it, take all of me, take me to pieces.' But I could only watch her standing in a bath half-filled with soapy water, pale arms turning to tiger-stripes under the methodical slash of her blades. 'Aren't you going to do something?' she screamed. But what could I do?

'I sometimes worry that I'll never feel any kind of intensity outside sex,' she told me later, sat on the bathroom floor, the solitary shadeless bulb making blatant light of walls, bath, sink, her. Her clothes folded so precise on the toilet seat beside her, as if she'd taken them off before going to bed and left them ready for the following morning. All things she did - the way she carried her body, the way words parted her lips, the way she held a beer can or a coffee cup or a blade - carried with them an air of deliberation, as if her entire life had been a conscious build up to each sequential moment as it unfolded.

Ten years on from Louisa. I sit in my flat, arm a mess of bleeding, listen to Patsy Cline. Walking After Midnight. I smoke a cigarette. Stub the butt. Gulp down my anti-mad pill with a mouthful of beer, sugar of fermented hops masking its acrid taste. What shall I do, now and next? Squares of sunlight on walls and floor, squares of sunlight over me and fading. Bye bye squares of sunlight. When do I cut? Are the parameters of my cutting fixed? Perhaps. I cut when I miss the world that presses in around me. Know that affiliation or blithe attachment is decay. Move on, with diligence. Move on.

'I don't know how you can fancy me,' Louisa said.

'Why?'

'Because I'm fat and ugly and my tits are too big. I'm a bloated psycho bitch.'

She pulled her knees in tighter, stubbed out her cigarette. A roll of belly slipped out from her control.

'Do you want to fuck me again?' she said, and smiled, put on a Pixies album.

I've been getting very forgetful of late. I might have mentioned that. It's probably because of the pills. I wasn't forgetful before, and I recall reading that such symptoms can be side-effects of the medication. There's a certain irony in the fact that the pills make me absent-minded, which means that sometimes I forget to take them.

I make contracts with myself. Here's an example. If I get home and Shell has left a message on my ansaphone, I'll not cut tonight. If she hasn't, I will cut. To cut, or not to cut, has nothing to do with her. 'Do I cut tonight, or not?' I ask myself, don't think I'm in any fit state of mind to make that decision right now, don't know what criteria I should employ to make the assessment. So I defer it elsewhere. Something else can make it for me. Future closing itself off from view. Beer, let's have another.

5am once, I found Louisa on the kitchen floor, sweeping up broken glass, tears fat on her cheeks.

'I'm sorry,' she said, 'I broke your favourite glass. I didn't mean it. I don't deserve you. I don't deserve anything.'

'What are you doing still up? I woke up, thought you were sleeping, hours ago.'

'I couldn't sleep and was thirsty and went for some water and dropped the glass. Then I wanted to use the glass to cut myself up because I'd broken your favourite and I don't deserve you.'

'Why don't you deserve me? Of course you deserve me.'

'You say that so easily. So fucking easily. It doesn't work like that, though,' she sputtered, pacing the room and looking for things to throw. And I couldn't help but see sexy in the tension of her limbs. Two days before, she'd found a piece of paper which read, in my handwriting, 'She loves me to the point of suffocation.' 'Is this about me?' she asked. 'No,' I said. 'I'm just your fucking abortion,' she said, and we fought then, too. Her mouth squeezed into a hard pink line. She hit me and I hit her back, she shouted 'misogynist, woman-hater', ran to the bathroom. She'd have loved a bruise on her face, I thought after, so she could say to her friends 'there, see, see what he does.' I, too, had no bruise. Hug, not fight, I always worried, and besides there seemed little else I could do with her. She back from the bathroom and my arms around her, into the bedroom and we lay on the bed; there, in the pool of her defences, of her sadness. My body such clay as I reached out to the bookshelf, took down a volume and we turned the pages together; An Encyclopaedia Of Things That Never Were. She loved that book.

'It's so cool to be on antidepressants these days,' my friend Matilda says, 'everybody's doing it. Even my mum and my kid sister. Most of the people I went to Uni with are on them. And the doctors don't care, they'll dish them out to anybody who asks. But maybe they understand it more than I'm giving them credit for. The doctors, I mean. They know it's a fashion thing. A lifestyle choice.'

As it was for me, as I try to explain to her, before giving up and copping off with somebody instead. Probably Jill. The lifestyle I choose is simple, its fashions direct and to the point. I want to be able to get up for work in the morning, go to work, come home, eat, pass the evening, go to bed, and repeat. I want to be able to function.

I once made Louisa stand in front of the bathroom mirror. She bruised like a messed up thing. Big body making shivers. Limbs covered with scabs and hairline scars.

'Look at yourself,' I said. 'What's wrong?'

'I can't do this. It feels bad.'

Looking in the mirror too, me her lover. I ran a finger up the torso she held tight in fucking, the arms she used for hugging, the lips she thrilled at in kissing. Could never shave without missing some. Felt more like a shaky child than anything approaching adult.

'I'm getting cold,' she said. 'Throw me that tee-shirt.'

'Just a minute.'

'Look, I'm getting goosebumps.'

And she pulled a tee-shirt over herself; mine, Swans, black and baggy to her thighs, then walked out of the room. I wanted her to tell me all the things that ever hurt her; instead we opened some beers and discussed favourite serial killers, a trick my father taught me. Wanted to open my veins, a way of being open for her, wanted to stand her in front of the mirror every day until she accepted that she was sexy.

I admire my blades. I respect their power. Not a power they have over me, more a power that is latent within them. A part of me says that I shouldn't need to cut. I know that. I'm not stupid. Another part of me says that there's no reason why I shouldn't cut. I oscillate in the dichotomy. Words are only thoughts, caught in the process of movement. Much can be yielded in the veneration of a leaf, of a second, of a blade.

I didn't cut when I was with Louisa, alone or in her company; faced with the frankness with which she approached it, her blatancy, I couldn't bring myself to.

'I was on Prozac for over a year,' my friend Jess says. 'At first I couldn't think bad thoughts. After a while I couldn't think at all.'

Louisa was sectioned. I got home one evening to our stale rooms, and to a message on my ansaphone. She'd named me as next of kin which I found a bit odd since I'd dumped her, mad at her madness, and hadn't seen her for more than two weeks. Perhaps she just wanted me to know of her latest escapade; here I am, it's cool and bloody, where is my mind, you'd like it here.

But, she was sectioned. What facts are there? Apparently she'd been to see her doctor for one thing or another, something banal, a smear or some such, she'd got tired of sitting around and tried to set light to the waiting room before slicing herself up in the presence of an almost full reception.

Louisa, go for it.

I went home, stared at the thread-bare laces of my boots, didn't know what to do. Looking back at the rooms through which we'd moved, it seemed I could barley have been there. It could have been anybody, that comforted and hugged and strove to love Louisa. Did we love? I think so, but don't know if I feel the evidence.

City adrift under a smooth blur of rain. I catnapped in order to dream. Woke up late with only a few hours of daylight left. Masturbated to nothing in particular. Wondered where our bodies end. Ransacked my mind for anything. Rubbed my sleep-rimmed eyes. Spent five minutes trying to remember what I intended doing. The rain-soaked window distorted the view outside. Buildings became grotesque shapes, streetlights balls of fire. I smashed a glass, drew knives of glass down my arms. The blood and the bleeding left me clean. I could sleep then, slept the sleep of one utterly at peace with all creation. Didn't worry for Louisa. The tucks and folds and curves of her, the form I held and caressed and entered and held briefly as holy, but which she only despised. Rain making nails on the window. Blood quickening on my arms. There are always other lovers, other bodies; to conquer, and fuck, and forget in. I don't know where Louisa is now. I logically assume that she's dead.

3.

'I thought you weren't going to call me.'

'I said I would,' Shell says.

'But people don't.'

'Well I have. I've been busy. I'm sorry. But anyway...'

I meet Shell the next evening, in a Greenwich riverside bar I used to come to sometimes with Suzanne, in the days when Suzanne and I went drinking. Shell seeks out a table by a window looking onto the water. The heat so intense that the river shimmers beneath us. I wasn't sure how to greet her, if we should kiss or hug, and we did neither, she smiling slyly before backing into her chair, and I thought it odd; we'd already slept together yet now felt physical strangers. So we make small talk and drink, and laugh; mainly on eighties cinema, which I discover she's quite a fan of. Bladerunner and Excalibur are her favourite films.

'There's something I need to talk to you about,' I say. 'I cut myself. I'm a depressive, and I cut myself.'

'I just want to help you,' she says. 'I know you've got issues. If you need my support or my help then you've got it. No rush. In your own time.'

She puts her arms around me, pulls me toward her. The sun, city-haze and river burn with the intensity of a Turner painting. I nuzzle into Shell's neck, look across to the opposite bank.

'Shall we go back to yours?' she says.

I have favoured blades. A few years back I was temping for an advertising company, opened a drawer in search of correction fluid, beheld a sheaf of scalpel blades, artists' slicers intent for card, and I knew I had to claim them as mine. Theft, I know, but they were bespoke for me, for the job I had in mind for them. I dislike razor-blades. Too frail, too flimsy, too much of a cliché; they don't sit comfortably in my fingers, inapt for the work I wish to put them to.

I like to look at my wounds. My wounds are beautiful. They make me so in their healing, make me want to search out vacant skin for further cutting, make me pick a path between scabs and scars. But cutting isn't gratuitous. Sometimes I take up a blade, pinion it between my fingers, put it down again, know this is not the right time. A few seconds or minutes from now, or won't you come back tomorrow. The hardest part of thought, I've found, is deciphering what is me and what is advert, what is TV, what is movie dialogue, what is conversation I overheard on the home train, what is song lyric.

I keep looking at the bathroom wall, expecting to see a clock. A clock hung there when Suzanne called this room her bathroom. Suzanne doesn't live here any more. I know this but need to remind myself. The face in the mirror lies to me. It tells me I am one thing. I know I am another.

Who is she, this Shell that shares my bed? Now that we have shagged again, am I supposed to have any sense of her? I know her name, know her cinnamon smell, know the knotty topography of her body. Know that she cries when she listens to Nick Drake, know that Brazil is the only film we could agree upon as great, know the veins that line her temples when she comes. Imprint of our bodies on sheets and on each other. But who is she? What is her identity?

I scrape a scab from the back of my wrist; it falls belly-up like a dead insect.

What am I doing in this room? It's my kitchen. I haven't switched on the light yet. I'll do that first. Why did I step in here? I'm sure there was business to attend to. The washing up needs finishing, the surfaces wiping, there's a kettle so perhaps I was keen on coffee. There's beer in the fridge, so I might have gone for another. Maybe if I step out of the room and come back in again, I'll remember what it was I was supposed to be doing here.

Cutting isn't a consuming occupation. Don't recall the moments with clarity, only the details. Where I was, the time of day, the degree of light, which song soundtracked, which implement I used (latest - home and living room and sat at desk, not quite twilight, desk lamp on and other lights off, Three Days by Jane's Addiction, instruments the usual). At the time it made sense for me to take a blade and push it into the skin of my arm. Felt familiar, like reaching out to an old friend. With retrospect, a fuzzy logic sets in.

I tell myself that I can take or leave cutting, but once you get into the habit it's hard to still it. Matilda once told me 'there's no such thing as an ex-alcoholic. There are only resting alcoholics.' The same is true of cutters. All cutters know that the sensation never leaves. It merely hibernates, incubates, waits until the arrangement of one's life is such that it can manifest again. A sense of anticipation sets in. Sometimes at work I go to the toilet, enter a cubicle, roll up my shirtsleeve and admire my scabs and scars. They please me, make me want to give them companions. Four or five nights back I was standing at a bus stop, headed home after visiting Matilda. Had a blasé annoyance at the lack of a bus. Knew that I'd put on music when I got home. Considered the music, perhaps Iggy or Velvets, was undecided. Knew I'd sit at my computer, knew I'd read my email, knew I'd cut. I was resigned to this schedule, had no quarrel with it. Was eager for the bus to hurry so that I could cut. I passed the bus-wait, waxing. Thought on my blades, the angle at which I'd hold, the glad blood that would blossom. Habit kissed off. City out of sight.

Shell doesn't mention my cutting, even though I'd told her it was a thing I did and didn't feel the need to mention it after the sheared statement of that fact. She skirts around it, in the same way that during sex her fingers brush my scabs without touching them.

Points in space and time are all that exist. The rest is just dressing.

Do I really believe that? I'm not sure. I can seldom focus on a single thing for long enough to formulate a belief about it.

But still a great notion. Still always sometimes a great notion.

Coffee. That's what I need. Perhaps a cigarette. I need a cigarette. And beer? A beer. Maybe I should call Matilda, see what she's doing tonight. Maybe I should go out, or maybe I should know when to stay in. Get things done. Maybe I should check my email. Visit some bookmarks. Read. Functional plans. Maxims. That's what I need.

I pick my scabs some more, a way of letting me bleed without cutting.

This universe that creaks and groans, this universe that stutters and suffers, this universe that seethes and heaves outside of me. I have intentions. I have designs for it. A plan to fuck with the blueprint. I lie awake at night and plot routes of escape.

I see Shell two times a week, sometimes three. We usually go for a drink or to eat or to see a film, before retreating to her flat or mine. Our time then divided between fornication and chess, because aside from sex and food/drink/film, we don't have much in common. Shell, how is it for you?

It's the tail-coat of August, and a Friday. Fridays used to be an out with my friends and getting drunk and copping-off night. Shell and I are in her flat, lying naked and half-covered by a sheet, the bed below us soaked with sweat. Stuffed animals gaze down at us. It's almost too hot to move. Shell hasn't said anything for a while. I got here from work, via home to change from my suit, and we had sex. She was attentive, meticulous yet with a lack of passion, as if she were doing it for my benefit, to lift my mood. Maybe she was. And now we watch the room slowly shift into night; a gradual mutation, but if you switch into the process you can see it and follow it as it happens. Bassy throb of music from the flat below. The TV is on, one dating show or another, mute but we're not really watching it. I want to go for a drink, beer to ease the heat, soothe the sweat that forms a second skin on me.

'How was your day?' she says, pushing the sheet down with her feet.

'The usual, really. How was yours?'

'The usual.'

I rest my hand on her belly, mouth open against her navel as if ready to whisper all my secrets to the flushed cavity of her womb. But I

31

don't have the words.

'Do you fancy going out for a drink?' she says.

'We could do. If you want.' I lift my head.

'Yeah. It involves getting dressed, though, and I don't know if I'm too hot to get dressed.'

'You could go as you are.'

'Yeah, right.'

'You'd have no trouble getting served.'

She pulls her knees up, hooks her palms around her calves, says other stuff. I listen but don't feel like I'm there. Stare at the potted plant on the window ledge. Impossible to tell if it's plastic or seed-grown. I know I ought to be able to know the difference, but I don't.

'Let's do it,' she says.

I watch Shell as she moves around the room, gathers up her clothes, collects mine too and tosses them onto the bed.

'Did I tell you about what happened to my friend Lucy from work?' she says. 'She'd been to visit a friend of hers who lived in a tower-block, she was leaving the building - it was about midnight by then - she heard a big crash, looked over and somebody had jumped off the building, landed about ten feet away from her. Some guy who'd just split up with his girlfriend.'

'Jesus.'

'Yeah. He was only in his twenties. She said that at first she didn't even realise it was a person, thought it was a bag of meat somebody had thrown out of a window or something. Bet that cheered you up, didn't it? Not that you needed cheering up. Or maybe you did. Let's go to the pub.'

Wounds heal. I check mine several times daily, pick at the scabs to prolong them, to make scars. Scars are good, a reminder. Each cut makes me stronger, confirms my dominion. I don't do it because I enjoy it. Pain has never been a friend of mine.

When I become aware that my mind has strayed, I cut to latch it back to its original position. Cutting gives punctuation, a place to be. When I cut, or drink, or fuck, objects cease to be objects. Cease to sit outside and beyond me, glow with a soft yet palpable significance. I like cutting for its literalness. A series of points along a curve. An easily planned trajectory. I know what I do it for, know what I can get from it. It is a fair exchange. There is no hidden agenda. Cutting can be poetry, in the same way that mathematics can be poetry.

4.

I'm staggered, am on a dance floor, am bleeding. What happened?

September's here again; snorting coke, and playing games with friends. Jess and Matilda, as usual.

'Hey Matilda who's round is it?'

'Yours, no, Jess most likely, has he ever fucking bought you one, I mean, ever?'

'Where's Scott? You seemed so lovesick and wrapped, last time.' Scott is the boyfriend upon whose arm Matilda hang last weekend.

'I gave him the night off,' she shrugs.

'What does that mean?'

'It means I dumped him, and that everybody knows it except for him.'

'More charlie?' Jess tosses me his wrap, says 'Take what you want,' and I retreat to the toilet for a line or two.

'Are you on the pull tonight?' Matilda asks.

'Possibly. Why? Are you?' I say.

'I should be so lucky,' Jess says.

'Jess, quit waiting for something to happen,' Matilda or I say. 'Just go for it.'

Stefan was the first other cutter I met. I wasn't a cutter then. He was older; me sixteen, him eighteen. His room as frayed and as bare as a cheap hotel. He showed me his collection of razorblades.

'This one's my favourite,' he said, but to me it didn't look any different to the others.

'Don't you ever wonder what's inside bodies?' he said. Us both with elbows on the window-ledge, watching people and traffic pass outside, Bauhaus on the stereo, tinny as a cheap transistor radio; Mask, or probably The Sky's Gone Out, I don't remember.

'I mean, I know there's blood and flesh and muscle and bone,' he said, 'but what does it all look like? What does it all mean? Don't you wonder that, want to dig inside and see what's underneath? Or do you wonder whether it's the fact that we've got bodies that are the problem?'

'But that can't be the problem. If we didn't have bodies we

34

wouldn't exist.'

'But...' he said, 'but... but... I always saw my body as something other, something I was inside of, only in the same way as I'm in a room, never saw it as part of me. Sometimes, even, it seemed the cruellest joke. You mean I must live inside this thing, that this flesh and me are indivisible?'

'What body would you rather have?' I said, wonder how many others had heard this particular recital, sure it or variations upon it were a tested chat-up routine.

'You're missing the point. It's not a question of wanting any particular form, just that... body and self are so segregated. We need to blur the distinction. Need to reunite the two. Have you heard of John Fare?'

'No.'

'He was an artist. Mid seventies, I think. He arranged a series of performances, and at each one he'd get more and more of his body removed. Hacked off surgically, I mean. He's something of a hero of mine. Although his motives are entirely different, I can't help but admire his technique. He was driven primarily by art, I think, though my motives are purely spiritual.'

'Your motives for what?'

'Are you scared?'

'Scared of what?'

'Of course you're scared. Everybody is scared. People are born in to scared. You're so used to it.'

'Scared of what?'

'You tell me.'

'So what am I scared of?'

35

He picked up a razor-blade, his favourite, placed it against his arm, smiled, pushed; blood splashed hard onto window-ledge and hazel floorboards between us.

Matilda introduces me to Josie, her flat-mate. I've known Matilda for more than two years, and until tonight I never knew she had a flat-mate, thought she lived alone. Guess I should visit her place more often. Josie and I chat, flirt a little. Fun but throwaway. I fancy her, inevitably. I sense a glimmer of something in her eyes and her smile that indicates that it may be reciprocated. No matter. Skimpy blue denim jacket. Crotchet voice, skin and hair that might as well be heavenly. I imagine her pressed against me, fuck-mad and phantom, dissolve it. It isn't a concern. I enjoy the lightness. Matilda buys another round, we'd forgotten Jess just got one, and now the table bristles with glasses. We'll drink them all before too long.

'You've missed a bit,' Matilda says, pointing at Jess' so-lately shaven head.

'It was bad,' a guy to my left is bawling in somebody's ear, 'It was so bad, and I had to quit. My boyfriend was dying and I didn't know what else to do.'

I try to focus on where I came from, but where I came from invariably means my parents, which downs me further. The detail blurs, like a document photocopied over and over, until it muddies itself to the point of meaninglessness. Give me another beer. Fuck them. They're not me. People. They're not me. My Father. Who was he? His heavy

36

spunk put he here. My mother. Who was she? Outside of her womb, the hole that spat me, what was she? She was working in a shop. I know that. She must have wanted more. I would, if I were her. Some people claim to want sprogs only, that if they can reproduce they'll be happy, in the knowing that they've left something of themselves in the world. But people lie, and besides, it was never Mother's style. In comparison with my memories, it seems trite. She'd have got depressed, as she came home and fed her spawn. She'd have cried into nights so winsome. What was she keen on, before I happened? She always accessorised in most recent fashions and hairstyles. Was keen on the latest songs the radio offered, enjoyed them purely for their newness. Did she like sex? Was the fuck that begat me a good one?

Stuff happens; primarily, a lot more getting smashed. The coke sends me gnawing at my jaws. Movies flicker in my head. Like matter I am strange, am charm.

'It's a real zen thing,' Jess yowls in my ear.

I don't much care for the fact that I have to get up tomorrow, that I'm allegedly working. Five or so hungover hours seems a small price to pay for the good I'm feeling now. En route to the toilet I meet a face familiar, a second- or third-last shagged, can't remember her name. I'm sure my recent slept-with sequence runs thus: Suzanne, then Shell, then Kim, then x goth queen, then Jane, then Shell again, then entropy. Yet this face so fuck-off gorgeous is none of these people. I tell Matilda about this, she laughs, and we snog in a drunken kind of way.

'Oh god,' she says, 'I know I'd said we'd already almost broken up, Scott and me and that I mean, but that's not on,' so we laugh to dissolve it, make it a caned and between friends kind of thing.

'Fuck it,' she says, 'are we dancing tonight, or what?'

I only saw Stefan once or twice after that first cutting time. So wayward in my moods then, so blinkered in self, and didn't know the autonomy of medication. I'm consistent in my habits, if nothing else. I wasn't consciously avoiding him, more that we were seldom in the same places at the same times. I wasn't that bothered. Even I saw him as unhinged.

I look in the direction of the dance floor. See Jess there, see people there, see the flickering motive forms of them. They look so good and I suddenly want to be there too, but I'm too busy with Bowie songs looping through my brain. Who's that fucker Matilda is snogging? See the knot of his hands, the lank cowl of his hair. And Jess is dancing, too, on the other side of my vision. Maybe I should interrupt him, pilfer another line. I consider cutting but don't know who I'd be doing it for, my friends for neglecting me (cutting in a teen goth kind of way), myself (cutting in a post-teen goth kind of way), Suzanne who dumped me (cutting in a Poe kind of way).

'More drinks?' Matilda says, beside me. 'That's what this scene needs. More drinks.'

'I thought you were skint.'

'Maybe, perhaps, but there's always money in the world for

beer. That's where all these Third World countries are going wrong.'

'Who were you snogging?'

'Fuck knows.'

'I wasn't smiling at you,' says a woman aft of me. Ox-eyed, hair the red of a Coca Cola logo. Sexy in an absent kind of way.

'No? That's a shame. You've got a very nice smile.'

'Sorry,' I say. 'It's the pills. Makes me smile at anything that flies.'

'Know the feeling,' she says, strobe-lights flickering at her shoulders like seraph-wings, 'You're up too, that's cool.'

'Different pills. Pills that make me happy, my doctor reckons. What's your name?'

'Anne. Is this your regular haunt?'

'Sure. I'm something of an adept.'

'Adept' is a good word, I think. Right now, I like that word. It confers. Makes simple. The dance floor is simple. My stubble is simple, too. The fact of my stubble, the detail of my having driven a razor against my cheeks this morning. It's there. It exists. Exists in the same way the pulsing bodies around me exist. The music is a cascade of shapes. All these people looking to get laid. Whatever. No guide pegs. Where did I go then? I know I went somewhere. Where did Anne go?

I remember with absolute clarity the time I first cut myself. I was sixteen, still living with my parents. It was St Swithin's Day. I was in my room, my parents next door, the narcotic drone of their television through the wall. Books, clothes, records, scattered on the bed and the floor. Room turned orange by the sun that dipped at the horizon.

Much as I hate to admit it, much as it sounds so clichéd and so blatant now, the scene was soundtracked by Joy Division's Closer. Ten or so years on it would have been Nine Inch Nails, or Placebo, or Manic Street Preachers; Richey era, anyway. No mind. These things happen. At least it wasn't The Smiths, or one or another forgettable eighties goth band.

I'd been for one of my walks. Felt alone, untethered from the world. Wanted to cry, but didn't, or couldn't. And it all seemed so simple. Cut yourself and you'll feel better. This is the way. Step inside. I took a disposable razor, cracked open the plastic casing to extract the blade. Held it against my arm. Pushed and dragged. All my energies channelled into that methodical act. After the flush of splitting skin, so many things shifted into focus. Brief glimpse of pink flesh glistening underneath, of inside me, before the blood welled. I stared at the cut for several minutes, watched my blood pulse thick as come, saw it congeal. Had no words. Felt clean, knew that cutting was the way to go, that my life could never be the same. It was like discovering masturbation. Through cutting I slept better, studied better, anguished better. Whatever words I conjured, they were flowers in deserts of dust.

'Things change,' somebody nearby says, 'has nobody ever told you that?'

Her hair is blonde. Her hair is purple. Hello? Do I know you?

Jess, where are you? Matilda, where are you?

I head to the toilet, select an empty glass from a table on the way. Go into a cubicle, pint glass in hand. If I cut myself this moment will reveal its significance, will unlatch all the things it can be, all the things it can give me, all that lurks beyond me. I place the glass on the floor. I wait for the room to empty so nobody will hear the slam of my boot on the glass, won't know as I stoop and pluck the sharpest fragments.

My parents never knew. I hacked and cried and bled in my room and they never knew. Sliced, squeezed my arms to extract every drop, always careful not to splash on floor or furniture or clothes. Cutting is one of the easiest of manias to hide. Then, as now, some days I'd cover my scabs with long-sleeves, other days I'd not care who saw them as long as it wasn't my parents or teachers. Anybody else was insignificant, wasn't my problem.

And then I'm on the dance floor, Jess on one side of me and Matilda on the other. I'm dripping blood between beats, each drop so perfectly matched. Where's my beer, Matilda? Who's round is it, Matilda? I light another cigarette. The world is drunk, not me. The world is depressed, not me. The world regrets, not me. The world cuts, not me. Life is good, and wondrous, and elsewhere.

'Group hug,' Matilda says. 'Let's get you out of here.'

Outside the club, I stand waiting as Matilda hails cab after cab until one stops. I want to tell her that I don't care if the cab stops or not.

'What happened to Jess?' I say.

'He's still inside. His turn next time. To take care of you, I mean.' And she smiles.

I smile too, gaze up at the broken sky. The rain falls only for me.

'I'm sorry,' I say, a phrase that has figured much in my life of late.

'You don't need to be sorry,' Matilda says, 'You just need to be happy and sensible. Come on. Let's take you home.'

5.

Hello blades. Hello sensibility. My flat looks like an abattoir. Hyperbole, I know, but there's blood on walls and floor. I'm sure there'd be blood on the ceiling too, if I was tempted to make the effort. Whatever. The near-full moon is my friend for tonight, and the universe is a wondrous thing. See it there, the moon, in the nook of the window, parting cloud and letting its light fill my room. Efficiently drunk, I turn a piece of paper in my hands. Creased and torn from an A6 lined notebook, Cassie's name and number scrawled there, in her elegant yet pointy script.

Cassie is the most curious case I've seen. Where most people might content themselves with mere slicing, she'd incise words into herself. The healing has rendered them partly legible; the only word I could make out was 'exit', scribed inches above her left wrist. We met at a party. Cassie by the door of a blue-walled room, seated in a circle of beer-cans and candles. Red hair crimped to her cool hips. Spiralling knot tattoo, bracketed by a lattice of scars covering most of her arm. I don't know how far they run; her tee-shirt obscured the boundary. She lit a cigarette, smiled but only for herself. Beside her a lanky oriental man, his eyes a ketamine stare. 'Is that your boyfriend?' I said, and she gave a neither 'yes' or 'no' shrug, so I asked 'Are you right-handed?' 'How do you know?' She fingered her nose-ring. Her lips shone like blood. 'No scars on your right arm,' I said. She said 'Oh. Okay. I'm sorry. Whatever. I'm not very good at conversation when I'm drunk. The only conversations I can really do then are the ones all about how pointless drunken conversations are.' She smiled then, and I fell for her.

I was told yesterday that Jesus loves me. I didn't know her, the bringer of those words, yet she seemed so sure in the knowing and the need to share it. Her face lined and freckled, shirt blue-pale and clear as water, her hands making birds in the air as she spoke. Though gratified at the knowledge, I was a little put out by it. Where was I when this decision was made? Where was my say? Why was I not consulted? I wish Jess had been there at the time. When I told him about it afterwards he said 'A while back I came to the conclusion that Jesus doesn't love me at all. He says he does, but really he just uses me for sex.'

I should address some practicalities, don't know how much detail I need to give. I cut deep enough to draw blood, but not to a degree that requires bandages or stitches or surgery. The blood can easily be washed away, the wounds treated - if I can be bothered - with a swab of disinfectant. Yes, the next day I have scabs. Yes, with time they become scars. I used to wear long sleeves until the healing was done, but now I generally don't bother. People don't notice. A few nights back I saw my friend Robbie. It took three hours of us sitting at the same table, drinking and talking, before he said, 'Jesus, what's that? Have you been cutting yourself?' I mumbled something along the lines of 'that's one of the reasons why I'm on antidepressants', a standard lie when I don't feel able or willing to explain; the two - pills and cutting - are interlinked, but do not have a correlation. 'You could have been a bit more imaginative,' Robbie replied. 'They're all going in the same direction. How about a cross-hatch, or something?'

'I'd like to see you again,' I said to Cassie; smiles unafraid, suck her breath, our mouths inches from each other's but still unkissed. Adore there. Your hair is beautiful tonight; what more can a song lyric say? Perfection. 'You're thinking about something,' I said; 'What are you thinking about?' 'I'm trying to decide if I'm single or not,' she said, 'I'm trying to decide how much I want to be single or not. What about you? Are you attached?' 'No. Yes. Sort of. I was. I still kind of am, in a way.' She shrugged caned, sunset-smiled, said 'We could just be friends. It'd be good to be friends with you. I think we could be very good for each other as friends.' 'We could,' I said; cigarette in one set of fingers, beer can in the other. 'And you're right. I think we would, too. But do you think that's going to happen?'

I'd like to think that after an evening's cutting, I go to sleep sated. Sometimes, but it isn't that clean. Some nights it fulfils, other nights I wonder why I bothered, feel like a fifteen year old in the self-imposed seal of their bedroom, listening to Nine Inch Nails and decorating their limbs with blood. But how else can I get outside me? I'd like to know. I've worked all the suggestions and they leave me so lacklustre, with such a sense of imprecision. If I'm a fifteen year old Nine Inch Nails fan, so be it. I can think of worse things to be.

I glance from the phone, to the moon, to the paper-piece in my hand, and back again. I know that if I call Cassie it'll be the instigation of something unstoppable, something iconic. I change the CD, Beck to Tom Waits, sip beer, pick up a lighter. Turquoise plastic disposable, Cassie's lighter, the lighter I pocketed that night we met, thinking for a second that it was mine. I strike it. No flame. Place it gently on my desk, don't want to bin it because it was once hers, is a tie to her as much as the paper-scrap that holds her phone number and email address. An object is nothing in and of itself. Is artefact, is residue of process, of time. I know this.

Cassie. Cassie. Cassie, Cassie, Cassie. Cassie and I didn't discuss cutting, that spotless night we met (except for my opening question, which I now see as rude in its directness, and for which I ought to apologise when I next see her), though it was clear that she'd noted my scars and scabs. It was part of the attraction, for me at least, maybe for her too, though it didn't seem worth mentioning. We were already more than that. 'I can't believe you haven't tried to kiss me yet,' she said, drops of liquid at the corners of her lips, shining like pieces of sky. 'But it would be a very bad idea, we both know that because we're both attached, so it's probably for the best.' She laughed and her laugh seemed the most profound thing I'd ever heard, so full of life. And I wanted to touch her, not in a sexual way but just to feel my hands resting on her skin, to feel the pulse of her aliveness beneath my fingers. Silver ring looped through her right eyebrow. The shadows on her taut arms. The scent of her hair, rich as honeysuckle. The angle at which she held her cigarette, or her beer-can. Details surrendering wonder, giving way to that point where meeting, or coupling, ceases to be person to person and becomes mythology.

I go out then, lose myself in city. In bars and in drink and in friends and in people who aren't yet friends but might be, given time. The city is the perfect conceit. Its lights so elastic, so electric and so magic. On the streets nobody knows my name, and nobody cares. I can be anybody.

Circulating

'Here,' Danny says, turning the car off the road and into a farm track. 'I've used this spot before.'

We glide to a halt under the cover of trees and he shuts off the lights. I look at the clock on the dashboard. It's a few minutes after midnight.

'Are you ready?' he says.

I nod. 'Have we got everything?'

He reaches over to the back seat, pulls out a bag. 'Of course. Let's go.'

Outside the car, he slings the bag over his shoulder. 'This way.'

The first thing that surprises me is how dark it is. I can see the silhouettes of trees and hedge-rows against the sky, a hill ahead of us, the glimmer of a town ten miles away. He starts walking, and I do my best to follow; slowly, unable to see my feet, testing each step before taking it.

'Don't worry,' he says. 'Your eyes will adjust.'

He's right. Soon I can make out his head and shoulders well enough to be able to follow them, to not have to rely on the sound of his boots. Looking down, I can even see where I'm stepping.

'I've hit this location before,' he says. 'We shouldn't have any trouble.'

I've only known Danny for a few weeks. We met online, arranged to go for a drink. He outlined his plan. 'Are you sure you want to do it?' he said. I nodded, and over a few pints we worked out the details. He sketched diagrams and made notes. 'When do you want to go ahead with it?' I asked. 'We can do it tonight, if you want,' he said. 'I've got all my equipment in the car.' 'Okay,' I said. We drove out of town, to a pub by a canal, sat in the beer garden and watched the sun set over Summer fields, waited for darkness.

We walk along the track in silence. I'm amazed at the sheer volume of stars that shine down at me. Am used to orange and soupy city skies, can't remember when I last saw so many. A crescent moon slides behind the horizon.

'It's a beautiful night,' Danny says. 'How are you feeling?'

'Nervous. What's that?' I turn; something rustles in the bushes to my right.

'Relax. It's probably just a fox. Are you sure you're okay?'

'Running on adrenalin. Let's keep moving.'

We soon pass a turn-off leading to a building with a solitary light on at the upstairs floor. It looks like a farm-house.

'This is where it gets interesting,' Danny says. 'The weekend before last, the place I was going to hit had a dog. It heard us, and barked it's head off and woke the whole house up. We had to abort. Too risky. We shouldn't have that problem tonight, though.'

We move as quietly as possible, until the house is far behind us. Danny stops, pulls a bottle of water from his bag. 'Want some?'

'No,' I say, reaching for a cigarette.

'Don't. It'll fuck up your night vision, and it'll give us away.'

At the end of the track, we come to a gate. My eyes have adjusted well-enough now, though I still see only in monochrome; wheat fields stretching away into darkness, a hill ahead of us.

'Get down,' I say, 'there's somebody up on that hill.'

'It's a tree. Anyway, even if there was somebody up there, they wouldn't be able to see us. You can see them because they're silhouetted against the sky. To them, looking down, they see only darkness. You do see people sometimes, though. Ramblers, people out walking their dogs. Once I came across a guy completely starkers, lying on his back in the middle of a field and looking up at the stars. I nearly tripped over him. The last one I did that I was telling you about, last weekend, we did have a couple of people on a hill above us. I think they were watching out for UFOs. The guys I was working with were getting off on it, I think, the idea that we might be spotted. They thought it added an edge to the proceedings. Anyway, we ought to get started.'

We climb over the fence and into a wheat field, follow the perimeter to a tramline. Take it, walk until we can only see crop around us.

'Let's do it,' he says. 'You remember everything I told you?'

'Sure.'

'We're keeping this one simple, since it's your first time and

49

there's only two of us. Seven rings, then we alternate the standing and the flattened bits, then the two circles on the edge. About two hundred foot. I need you to hold this for me.'

He hands me the end of a tape.

'Stay there,' he says. 'Hold it tight, and don't let your arms move about too much, or our circle will end up wonky.'

He walks until the tape is taut, then steps in a loping sideways gait through the crop. Marks out a ring around me, returns to where I'm standing. We walk to the perimeter of the ring he has trodden.

'Same,' he says, and marks out another ring around me. We move to the point where the two rings intersect, trace a third ring, then another where this meets the inner ring, another, then another. We return to the centre point. Danny opens his bag, takes out a length of board with string looped around it at either end, hands it to me.

'You know what you're doing with that?' he says, taking a second board from the bag. 'You take that bit, that bit, and that bit' - he points into the crop - 'and I'll do these bits. Remember the design? You know what bits you're leaving standing, don't you?'

I nod.

'Good,' he says. 'I'll meet you round the other side.'

I hook the board beneath one foot, hold the rope like reins, step forward, flatten a swathe of crop beneath me. I'm amazed at how loud it is, a deafening crunch as the stems go down. He'd warned me about this; 'it sounds loud because you're standing directly above it. To anybody on the edge of the field, it just sounds like the wind rustling the wheat-heads.' As I stomp my way through the crop, I'm not convinced.

By the time I start flattening a second segment I'm beginning to feel like I know what I'm doing. I strive to make the edges as precise as I can, then lay the rest of it in a loose spiral from the centre outwards. As I work, my adrenalin surges. I keep glancing over my shoulder and down the tramlines, expect to see a shotgun-wielding farmer advancing towards us. Somebody must have heard us, I think. Best just do this as quickly as possible, and get away from here.

Danny looms out of the darkness as I'm completing my third section.

'I've done the rest,' he says. 'We've just got those two circles on the outside. We'll take one each.'

He's finished before I've barely started, it seems, and stands in the tramline watching as I work. I flatten the last of the circle, collapse exhausted and sweating. My arms ache from holding the board, and my legs are sore from stomping.

'Let me just catch my breath,' I say, gulping down the water he hands me. 'It's tiring work. A lot more so than I was expecting.'

'We don't have time to hang around,' he says, tucking the boards back into his bag. 'Let's go.'

We don't speak as we walk back to the car. Once we're inside, and navigating narrow country lanes back to Danny's flat, he says 'So how do you think you did?'

'I don't know. How do you think I did?'

'We'll see tomorrow.'

I look at the clock. 'We weren't in that field for two hours, were we? It didn't seem that long.'

'It never does. Let's go and get some sleep. We'll come back and have a look tomorrow.'

Back in Danny's flat, I stretch out on his sofa. Flick through a book of pictures of circles, try to work out how they were made. They all look far larger and more complicated than I imagine mine was. I want to ask him about it, how he thinks ours will compare to the pictures, but I fall asleep with the book still in my hands.

The next afternoon, we drive back out. Park in the same spot as the night before, walk up the farm track to the field. I feel like a murderer. Stalking plants by night and taking them down, then going back the next day to survey the crime scene.

'I don't usually visit them after I've done them,' Danny says. 'I just wait for the pictures to appear online, and see what people have to say. But since it's your first one I figured you'd like to have a look. There it is.'

At first I can only see a dip in the crop, but as we make our way up the tramline toward it, it opens out, getting bigger, and I can see the overlapping rings and flattened segments we'd made the night before. We step inside, walk from one section to the next.

'Your first circle,' Danny says. 'What do you reckon?'

'It's bigger than I was expecting. And not as messy. This bit's quite messy, actually. I think it was the first bit I did. Who are those people?'

A middle-aged couple walk barefoot towards us. The woman holds dowsing rods in front of her. They quiver as she walks, cross when she reaches the centre of the circle.

'I like this one,' she says. 'Very gentle energies. Subtle but most invigorating.'

'Hello,' the man says. 'What do you think of it? It's a good one, I reckon.'

'It's a bit messy,' I say.

'Yes, but there have been quite a few people in it today,' the woman says. 'The broken stems were probably caused by them tramping about. Look at that bit over there.' She points behind us, to a section that Danny flattened. 'What a lovely, flowing lay. This is the real thing, definitely. There's no way anybody made this.'

'And it's aligned to that ancient site,' the man says. He points to a distant hill, where a group of megaliths stand silhouetted against the perfect blue sky.

'Did you know that was there?' I ask Danny.

'Of course I did,' he says.

'Anyway, we have to get going,' the man says. 'There's another formation on the other side of the hill we want to look at. Have you visited that one?'

'No,' Danny says. 'But I've seen pictures. It's a good one. Enjoy.'

'I want to stay in this one for a bit more,' the woman says. 'I need to realign my chakras.'

'Alright then,' the man says. 'We'll go to the other one later.'

Danny and I walk away from them, stand at the edge of the formation and watch the wind ripple through the wheat-heads.

'Realign her chakras?' I say. 'Was she for real?'

'Don't mock them,' Danny says. 'They can believe whatever they want.'

'But they're wrong.'

'Are they?'

'Of course they are. I know where this circle came from.'

'Can you prove it? And even if you could, where would that get you? You'd be prosecuted for criminal damage, and the mystery would be gone. Best just leave things as they are, don't you think?'

'Don't you feel guilty for deceiving them, though?'

'I haven't deceived anybody. It is what it is. Flattened crop. Those guys are the ones who are saying it's more than that, not me. It's a bit like those standing stones on that hill. People have wondered about that for years. Who built it? What's it for? They're still wondering. They come and see it and they marvel at the precision, at the geometry. I marvel at it, too. But somebody made it.'

I run my hands through the crop, feel the stems brush against my skin.

'It's addictive,' I say. 'I want to do another one.'

'You know how to now,' Danny says, by which I sense that he doesn't expect to be there the next time I'm in a field in the dark. He's just passing on knowledge. And I do feel as if I've entered into a secret society of sorts. The moon and stars chart our forays. We skirt out under their cover, make our names in wheat fields. By day, nobody knows we were there.

I glance back over at the couple. The woman stands with her arms outstretched, chants rune names.

'Come on,' Danny says. 'Let's leave them to it.'

Red Room

'I saw lights,' Laurie says, pulling herself out from sleep, legs bent up, knees to breasts, kicking at the duvet. 'There were lights, here in the room. I had no control over them. They were leading me somewhere and I had no control over them.'

I hold her until stillness spreads through her again, until sleep takes her back inside its space. Watch over her through darkness. Tuck the duvet under her chin, brush stray hair from her forehead, smooth her frown-lines and goose-bumps. I can feel every thought her mind creates, transmitted through her skin.

There's a red door at the end of a hall. Laurie's room. Paper flaking from the walls like burning skin. Sounds of dead days hidden beneath the floorboards. Unslept-in bed scattered with stuffed toy animals. Red hole through the carpet. She was made here. The dust of old skin is everywhere her bare feet tread. Carbon perforates the air she breathes. She closes the door.

We met at a fancy dress party where everybody came as aliens. The hosts, a crusty couple from Stoke Newington, were hand-in-hand greys. The walls painted with stars and spirals and goatsuckers and greys and double helixes and fractals. I was Mork. Laurie was wrapped in bacofoil and chatting to a man with a television aerial sellotaped to his head. 'I slept with Kali once, when I was tripping,' he said, 'Best shag I ever had.' Laurie and me stood on a balcony; we talked and passed joints between us, watched the city spread out beneath the sky, sky endless and broken with clouds and meagre stars. 'The stars know who we are,' Chewbacca said, putting an Orb tape on. Laurie and I went home together, and a month later she moved into my flat; 'Before I moved out of my place I piled all my furniture and things up in the centre of the room,' she told me later, 'I wanted to set fire to it but I couldn't. I took a photo of it instead.'

That photo is thumb-tacked to the vacant wall between two fly-smeared windows, alongside photos of our kisses and of Laurie's family. Distant lawn of cakes and chequered cloth and grandmothers and sandwiches. Her mother holding her against the sky. Her father swilling Coca Cola from a dented can, cigarette squeezed between his yellow-stained fingers.

'Where do you think the lights come from?' I ask. 'I don't know,' Laurie says. 'My dad always claimed to be a master of lights. He said he could control them. He'd be sitting in his room and they'd appear, at first they'd be moving at random but he reckons he learned to guide them with his mind. Sometimes I'd imagine him putting all his thoughts inside them, then sending them out through the window, out over the world to do his will.' She walks across the room, hands spread over the round of her belly. 'And he was obsessed with aliens. Even though he told me there was no such thing. He said he'd studied the whole subject thoroughly, and... and that they weren't aliens, that they didn't come from space.' 'Did you tell him about you and what was happening to you?' I say. She laughs, moves over to the window, gazes at rain hung on the pane, at the hundred tiny Lauries reflected back at her. 'Well according to him they've always been here. People once called them fairies or thought they were Gods. Then when people were obsessed with religion they called them demons, and now we live in an age of technology we call them aliens. That's what he said, anyway. Of course, I didn't really believe him. I've learned to take most of the things he said with a pinch of salt.'

Her body briefly tightening, before sleep loosens her. I hold her and her skin tingles under my fingers. Bed warm to us. I chart the dreams that roll behind the orbits of her closed eyes. Hold my mouth to her forehead and breathe her thoughts. 'The red room fills my dreams now,' she says, soundless lips parted to sleep, 'I can hardly close my eyes without being there. I don't dislike the red room, I guess I admire... It was always the lights that led me there. At first the lights were really exciting, like seeing fairies or Father Christmas, or having your toys come alive or something. But... sometimes I feel something, can almost hear breathing, think I see movements in the corners of my eyes but when I turn to look and see what it is there's nothing there. I don't know what's going on. Sometimes I remember things, like... I can see a figure standing over me, I'm lying down, and... I'm so small, I wake up in the night, and I can't move, I try to lift my arms but I can't. There's something kind of dewy dripping on my eye-lids. Three drops. I hear a voice, calming, and... Then I see the lights again, try to control them like my dad could, try to guide them away from me, sometimes it seems like I can, but... I don't want to go on with it but something compels me. I can't control it. I can't control the lights. I have to let them guide me. They lead me through the red door, and...' 'Where are you?' I say. 'I'm lying on a table,' she thinks, 'There's metal on my wrists and ankles. I'm bleeding. It burns. The room is very bright. I look but I can't see. I see metal. It's so bright in here, but... Metal. It's against my skin. There's a hard heavy feeling, my... belly... feels so full. Something's crushing down on my chest, like someone's sitting on me. I see a pair of eyes, dark eyes, so big... A tiny slit for a mouth... There's something bitter-tasting in my mouth, and then... After that I don't remember. A face trying to smile that doesn't look like it was designed to smile. The next thing I know, I'm lying in my bed again and it's dark, blacker than blindness, and...' 'What else?'

She's awake now. 'I always thought that as I got older, the red room would go away,' she says, 'But... Things kept happening. I told my parents but they just said I was probably imagining things, that all children imagine things, they told me that having an imagination was probably a good thing as long as I didn't let it get control of me, but... And then... One day when I got home from school there were two men in long black coats sitting in the kitchen drinking coffee. They asked me lots of questions. I told them I didn't know anything. They were strange. They didn't blink. Their movements were jerky. One had a drop of spit hanging from his lip which didn't fall the whole time. The other one had really long nails, flecked with grey, like the nails of a dead man. And when he took his hat off he was completely bald, even his eyebrows were shaven. They got into this shiny new car and drove off. Later, after they'd gone, my dad told me not to tell anybody about those people or about what was happening to me. He said he didn't trust them. I didn't trust them, but I didn't trust him, either. I decided I needed to get out as soon as I could. I left home when I was sixteen. As I got older I met other people, who said, "Don't worry, you're one of us. It's okay. We've all been through the same thing. In a way it makes you special." But that still didn't help. There's always another shadow.' 'What happened to your parents?' I ask. 'My mum left my dad while I was at college. She lives in Ireland now. My dad shot himself.'

I wake up from sleep without dreams. Laurie's skin smells of dead rooms and nicotine and static electricity. 'Come with me,' she says. 'I need to go back to the red room, but I can't do it on my own.'

Under a swollen sky, a house in a street like any street, repeating to the limits of the horizon. Boards nailed over doors and broken windows. Sounds of children playing, the buzz of cars, flies in sticky puddles. Scraps of paper flit through the air like giant moths. Power-lines bisect the sky. We prize a board from a window, the rust-heavy nails twisted against our strength but eventually they give. We climb through into a hallway. Globes of light lead us as we move from room to room. We find nothing but the motes of long-stilled years. Newspapers from the seventies, a single silver bracelet, bare boards and scratches in dust. We open a door to a flight of steps reaching up into darkness. Hear a sound like the speeded-up voices of children. Faint scent of vanilla. 'This way,' Laurie says, and we move upstairs, are greeted at each step by slight whispers of forms, shapes and contours too vague to delineate. They filter down the bent wooden steps, become scarce-visible vapours as they brush past our faces. I turn, caught in cold air, watch them disappear into the room from which we had just stepped. Hallway of shadows. Two doors to the left and two to the right. 'There,' Laurie says. The door is ajar. A shadeless bulb hangs lightless over a red-walled room. Peeling posters of seventies bands stuck with yellowed sellotape. Wooden frame of a single bed. Dismembered dolls scattered on the floor. A rotted half-eaten chocolate bar. Our eyes draining away the darkness. 'I can't go any further,' Laurie says. 'I feel sick. Sickness fills this place.' She curls on the floor outside, knees up to her face. I look at her then turn away, step into the inner skin of the room, stand at the end of the bed. See tiny rapid movements at the fringe of my sight; I turn, try to focus, see nothing there. I practice not focusing, not looking, letting the room reveal itself to me. The walls blur. Foundation shifts. The shadows are transparent. There's a ghost against the wall, a milky grey-skinned hologram of a little girl on grazed knees and a man standing over her. Her clothes on inside out and backwards. Her body curling out of him. He holds a finger to her lips. Snakes of blood wriggle between their bodies. Her skin flakes away under the scalpel of his fingers. Splinters of light shine inside her wounds. Coca Cola and semen seeping through her veins. Nothing inside his eyes can understand. White light flowing from his fingertips, swelling to a halo that surrounds them both. I turn and Laurie is beside me. The man stands tall, arms stretched at his sides. The girl falls to the floor, fades to a dull smear of calcium carbonate. Laurie's lips move before I hear any sounds; then twenty-five years pour from her, a deluge of half-shapen syllables. The light expanding over him, consuming him, growing to the torrent of her words, reclaiming her skin of stars. Then it is just a bedroom and Laurie and me, and the white stains of memory that seep through bare wooden boards.

The Golden Boy That Flew To Never

The walls of the room pulse rhythmically in the corners of my sight. Lydia moves between walls and me, sometimes fuses with cool wood and metal and concrete. I'm sitting by the bar. People fill the room all the way to the dance floor. Colour and light scamper in my veins. I watch the tight crowd centred on Lydia, the Euclidean forms of their sculpted bodies gliding at identical angles. The beat is solid matter under each of their movements.

'I'm not having the right number of orgasms,' one woman suddenly squawks; olive face, swarm of freckles. 'I was reading about it in this magazine. It left me feeling so inadequate, you know.'

'I don't think there is a right number,' a man to her right says, 'as long as you're happy with what you're having.'

'But doesn't it worry you that someone else is having more than you?' she says, 'I mean, don't you feel left out? Anyway you would say that, you're a guy.'

'Children, children...' Lydia says, pulls them both round to her. I listen and watch their lips move. Want to join the group but know I can't tell stories because I have so little memory. Don't recall even the simplest things I did or their sequence. Lydia away from the crowd now, throws some shade towards me.

'How's your evening going?' I say. 'I've hardly spoken to you at all.'

'Terrible,' she says. 'I spent far too long thinking about all the people I hated shagging. How are you? I'm glad you called me. I haven't seen you for ages. Where have you been?'

'A bit caught up in things. That looks like Ailsa.'

'Who looks like Ailsa?'

'Other side of the bar, but she's gone now.'

'Who's Ailsa?'

'Ridley's flatmate.'

'You miss him, don't you?'

'Of course I do.'

Lydia smiles, touches my arm, laughs, says 'you worry too much.'

She sneezes, blows her nose, snags the tissue on her nose-ring, says 'I haven't quite got used to it yet,' tucks the ring back into its hole. I smile too, flit in and out. Body here, head crossing continents. Can hear my cigarette burn down. Should travel more I guess. Maybe Tokyo. Ridley said he thought I'd like Tokyo. I look up from my glass and the insufficiently orgasmed woman is beside me, as if all the people in the room were slots in a puzzle Lydia had steadily manoeuvred until we were together.

'So what do you do?' she says.

'What do you mean?'

'Have you got a job?'

'Yeah. I work in an office. Admin stuff, boring.'

'I work in an office too, but not for much longer.'

'Why? What are you going to do?'

'I'm going to The Amazon. A friend has fixed it up for me. I'm going to be studying, what are they, yes... woolly spider-monkeys,' and I don't so much listen to her words as drift amongst them, her lips so full of purpose, she tilts her mass from one side of her body to the other as she speaks, the way Ridley would sometimes, saying 'it's the largest monkey in South America, apparently. And there's only a few hundred left, so we might not see any at all.'

She reaches for her drink and I wonder why we filled five minutes with the particular words we chose, if any random assortment would have used the time the same way.

'I won't remember you when I get home,' she says, turns away, ducks from Lydia's straying cigarette-hand.

Outside the bar, the street has saved cool air for us. Lydia holds out her hand as if anticipating rain, 'I need some junk' she says, buys a burger from a van on the corner, 'quick, there's a cab!' and we taxi to a room that smells of coffee and mint; Lydia's lounge. She hugs hello to her cats, pillows herself on star-shaped cushions.

'Where was Chloe tonight?' I say, picture Chloe in the corner of a room with a book in her hand and sweat on her brow, adjusting her tie and being Lydia's most beautiful girlfriend.

'Fuck knows. At home, I think. I don't know. I was supposed to call her, but I forgot. She's somewhere. It's not going to last.'

'I thought you really liked her.'

'Yeah, I do. That's the problem. Every time I get something good I want to fuck it up. I guess fucked up is what I need or look for in any given situation.'

In the bathroom I do my best to piss straight, before curling up on Lydia's sofa. My hands exist at several points at once. Lydia smiles, kisses my cheek, hands me a pint-glass of water, says 'I'm going to bed now, drink this before you go to sleep,' and she's gone.

I light a cigarette. Can hear every breath pushed out of me, feel it jagged in my chest. Water tastes good. I forgot how good it tasted. My clothes stay where they fall. I see Ridley in wallpaper patterns, his face turned away from me. Can smell the lavender scent that seeps through epidermis onto everything he touches, his voice a sound that whirs in a loop round my brain.

When I was a child, and it took little more than rain to make me happy, I dreamed the same dream every few weeks. A guide comes to me and takes my hand, leads me into welcome night. We slide through sky like whispers, watch the world spread open before us and ride each gleaming darkness. Toys and stuffed rabbit forgotten, my parents just a shadow. My guide and me are all that is real, our glowing bodies spread wide to take in the sky. Becoming mountains and plains and draining every ocean, the pulsing sky and all sand of the sea. My hands open out to take in the stars, with not even a thought for the bones in those hands, or a care for the folds and scars of the skin that binds them.

Friday again. Home from work by early evening. Some food passes through me. The city shines blue like I'm underwater. I listen to the Doppler shift of each passing vehicle. Open a bottle of wine and watch the news. I'll call Zoe in awhile. Take the wine to the bath, lie there drinking and thinking about Zoe and melting into the water. It's hard to believe Zoe exists when she's not my line of sight. Sometimes she seems just a sound, the two syllables of her name which I break upon my tongue and little flows from them but noise. Where is she now in her world? I know only the soft intersections where we meet, bathe, talk, make love, sleep, before we disentangle ourselves, ready to drift again. I pour more wine and sit staring at the shadows, find faces in the wallpaper. Ridley dances through my head, feet skimming a trail of hopeful from past, through present, into future. The last time I saw him -

we were sitting in his kitchen, television on in the background, I was trying to catch the newsreader's words but the volume was too low. On the screen, trees were falling and people were running in all directions. Fast cut to the newsreader, then a tanker leaking black into the sea around it. Outside, the sun shone calm through turning snowflakes.

'What time's your flight?' he said.

'I don't need to leave for another few hours,' I said.

Some people you need to know for a long time before you can feel close to them in any sense, others slip effortlessly inside your life until it feels like they've always been there. Ridley I knew barely two months.

Half an hour later, us standing on a bridge, the Thames slow below us, snow deliquescing on Ridley's clothes. He held a video

66

camera, walked to the edge of the bridge, picked his footsteps carefully. I was content, knowing that I was going to the other side of the world but that something of me was stored on the tape wound tight in his camera, not realising it was the other way round and me that needed to store memories of him -

I look up. Night has sneaked in, switched on the lights without me noticing. I drink another bottle of wine to see if it will take me to a place I'm not at already. Zoe said she'd stop by after work, I think. Until her photography pays enough, she waitresses at an all-night cafe. She should be here by one or two. That gives me five hours. I think I made a mess of things at her photo preview last week -

I'm sitting on a leather sofa. My pores open, skin oily and becoming, brain lubricated by alcohol. I can feel the hide of the leather soak through my clothes, can feel the pulsing flesh of the cow that once carried it. Photographs clog white gallery walls; Zoe's photographs. Men and women bob from side to side of the room, their mouths opening and closing. I know they're talking but can't hear the words, can only see their lips move, voices adrift like crossover radio. I don't want to move but brother my cup is empty, glide shape without form between groups of people, not seeing them, just the shapes that spaces make between them. Stuck-out shoulders collide with my every step. Can't see Zoe. The bar is a table against one wall, 'good evening sir, my name is Chantal, what can I get for you?'

Her mouth a downward arc, hair a skewered coil winding to the back of her head. The table a swim of styrofoam cups, open bottles of wine and beer, some cups already filled. I don't have to use words for this; look down, have one finger in a cup half-full with still

67

bloody liquid. I pick up the cup and Chantal smiles. Try to drink it slowly.

I can see Zoe now. She's talking to a man with greying goatee, her hands weaving air, guess he wants to fuck her, later she'll tell me 'he's a really important connection.' I find a space on the table for my drink, reach for cigarettes. The inside of my pocket is warm and dry. When I remove my hand the warm dryness follows. I put my cigarettes down on the bar. My vision blurred but I'll find them again because the packet is red and nothing else on the bar is. The room oscillates. Zoe talking to someone else now, she meets my glance sometimes. I open a box of matches upside down and they tumble to my lap. Reach for cigarettes, the packet dances across the bar and I follow it. Chantal stares, her smile chasing me, her hair slipping out of its coil and then the room is colour and texture and light I'm spinning legs dissolving

'are you okay?'

Zoe rents five rooms on the top floor of a Stockwell house; kitchen, bathroom, bedroom, lounge, hall, if you can count the hall as a room, which she does. Sitting on her sofa, cotton now, 'I can't fucking take you anywhere,' Zoe says.

She's standing by the door, room bent around her, her lips pushing out noise. People say drinking lets you forget but that's a lie, like a lover who offers to give up the sky to you. Drinking doesn't let you forget. At first it can dull the edges but that's only a false security. Zoe's cat strolls into the room. Black with white paws. Sits down. Licks its tail. Strolls out again. Sits in the hall. Licks its paws.

'Was it okay?' I say.

'Pardon?' Zoe.

'Your preview. Did they like your pictures? Was it okay?'

'Was it okay? What do you think? Tell me that. What do you think?'

'I don't know. I hope it was.'

'Well apart from you making friends with the floor...'

'Yeah, but...'

'But what?'

'But... seriously... I mean I bet most of them didn't even know you knew me, if... yeah? They probably just thought I was some drunken twat or something.'

'You were.'

'I've...'

'You've what?'

I give a sloppy shrug and Zoe walks out of the room. Her bones and fibre so comfortable inside her. Her cat meows to the tips of its whiskers and follows her. Through windows the city is a fuzz of light. In the room a table, three chairs. An ashtray. A bowl of pebbles and seashells. Camera. Wine glass. Three-dimensional jigsaw dilophosaur. All these objects waiting for people to pick them up and give them purpose. I follow Zoe's footfalls and the smell of catshit to the kitchen. She's scooping the contents of a catfood tin into a bowl. I open the fridge.

'You got any beer?' I say.

'You're taking the piss.'

'No, just something to level me out, that's all.'

Zoe doesn't answer, puts the bowl on the floor and phases out somewhere. I rock back and forth on my heels awhile, a habit I stole from Ridley, return to the lounge to chew my nails. Mad how we keep animals in our homes and feed them with food from tins.

'Why did you have to fuck it all up for me?' Zoe's words from somewhere. 'Really? I want you to think very hard about that. Not now but tomorrow. You think very hard about it. Okay?'

My mouth is dry. I drink water from a wine-stained glass. In my pocket five postcards of Zoe's photographs which she gave me the day after we met. Crumpled now. I smooth them. I met her a month ago or it could be three or weeks or whatever. Days and weeks and months disappear when you start to take drinking seriously.

'I can't talk to any of those people,' I say at last.

'Of course you can.'

'But where do the words come from?'

'What do you mean? What kind of thing is that to say? You just open your mouth and there they are. Anyway I'm not talking to you tonight. You're pissed. I refuse to talk to you when you're pissed.'

Into Zoe's bedroom. Four lillies drooping in a vase. Various bottles beside her bed, the creams and lotions she smears across her skin. I lie on the bed and watch the room orbit me. Zoe in the bathroom, the spiral of water into drain, the signature of her footsteps down the hall. Barefoot Zoe moving still-frame, white skin flickering, 'you're dribbling,' she says, I wipe my mouth with the back of my hand, watch her undress, her skin subdividing into zones of latitude.

'Goodnight,' she says, kisses my nose. I fold her into sleep and into me. More than content to remain a shadow for her, the rain that drifts in and outside when she sleeps.

'Attaining freedom is easy,' Ridley once told me, 'the difficult part is knowing what to do with it.'

Most nights, sleep takes so long to come. In bed, cigarette in

70

hand, staring at walls and ceiling and all the objects years have amassed around me. Lying beside Zoe, sometimes she couldn't even be there. All I know are the easy points of thighs, ankle, elbow where our bodies converge. I try to mimic her breaths, hope they will carry me into sleep with her but they won't. I get up. Align the postcards of her photos on the desk. Disturbed by their symmetry, I arrange them again by tone or by chronology or by subject. Zoe always sleeps with one foot sticking out from under the duvet. I met her at a party where a man was stabbed to death in an upstairs bedroom. The next afternoon was Zoe and me in my flat sharing wine and coffee and cigarettes, trails of our clothes winding from door to bed. Breaking up a carrot cake with forks. Viewing the world through small hands. Whisky bottle at an angle in my palm, brown flecks spotting the carpet. I try not to drink in front of her any more.

'Most of the time I look at the people around me and I feel like I'm a different species,' Ridley said. 'Do you know what I mean? Do you ever get that?'

Nothing is contained. I watch at the window to sodium blur and my lungs hang heavy in my chest. Sirens wail regular as hour hand. A spiral of orange peel reveals the place where Zoe sat.

Ridley died six months ago today. Each passing cab still makes me anticipate his footsteps at the door. Makes me anticipate his bright white turning fingers. Wipes his nose from the left side first. I think I lost myself somewhere along the line from that day to now.

Some nights my dream guide still comes. Takes my hand, pulls me up from my bed and we skate across the sky's belly of limitless blue darkness. Wings work at clouds. Weather plunges away. Below us I can see my flat, my empty bed with sheets twisted every way. The moon throws our twin shadows on rooftops and the long bare road. Land is endless lights on black for as far as I can see. We follow the bends of the river, out to the open sea. Not even a wind can blemish us.

There's so little of Ridley left. Isolated islands of memory, submerged a little further with each passing day. Some nights I try to recreate him. Write down the things I remember to stop them slipping away, let my pen follow time and gravity, my hand speeding up or slowing down at a rate determined by its angle to the page,

I met him in a bar, most people I know I've met in bars. 'I was supposed to be meeting a friend but she never showed,' I say, 'she's probably pulled somewhere.' Ridley's hands through his long hair, rings on every finger, he flickers like a black and white movie. Another time and place. Ridley walking silhouetted by sun. Swats a fly from his cheek. The arm-pits and spine of his tee-shirt damp with sweat. Ailsa, his flat-mate and sometimes lover, her grass-stained skirt wrapped round her legs by wind. That day, or the next. Sun turning everything to monochrome. I stand in the TV corner of the room. 'Most things I see make me want to put my foot through the screen', Ridley says, shifts his hips slowly from side to side, redistributing bodyweight from one leg to the other. Walks over to where I stand. 'I love the things sunlight does to the colour of skin,' Ailsa says. A beer getting warmer in my hands. 'I sometimes worry that anything human, any dream, is necessarily an act of destruction,'

Ridley says, strokes his palms, rubs a fingernail down the stunted lifeline, 'sometimes worry and sometimes simply don't care.' Ailsa is hands on hips against the wall, John Lennon singing and Ailsa's voice bleeds along, 'life is what happens to you while you're busy making other plans...' 'And sometimes in sex it feels like my body has ceased to exist,' she says, 'it's melted away, that's when I feel most real.' She cups her hands across her smooth round belly. Flaming star tattooed between her shoulder-blades. As the sun dips below the horizon the room becomes a fluid object. My mind dissolving, becoming matter in their hands -

pen down now, scribbled page in front of me that looks more like a stranger than Ridley. I can pinpoint little there of what made him unique, any different to the drift that anybody else made through me. The words simply can't see the point of him. I put the page aside and pour another glass of wine, stare at my filthy fingers. It's seldom a question of drinking for a particular reason; not because I'm happy or sad or celebratory or whatever thing, more a matter of letting alcohol become an accompaniment to more and more of the different things I do. It's like smoking, when I first started smoking I'd save each cigarette for a moment that best accompanied it, until that became any moment.

I didn't want to fall in love with Zoe at first. After our first day together I didn't expect to even see her again. But she phoned me a few days later and I didn't sleep for nearly a week. Lived a somnolent haze, read and drank and snatched Zoe where I could, usually nights after she'd finished work, and I worked too but made too many errors and dozed at my desk. It was a full two weeks before I saw her in daylight.

A month or whatever from meeting her. It's three in the morning or probably later, a Sunday becoming Monday. Another week of work. Another weekend done. Another afternoon of sick and wandering into things. Lydia carried me home or maybe a taxi, then a sleep and then another taxi to my Zoe.

Me by the window and Zoe on a chair in the centre of the room. She pulls out strips of negatives from a carrier bag, holds them up and squints to see what images they contain. Thumbs back her hair, murmurs 'no, that's no good,' or 'maybe', then drops them to the floor. A shapeless cardigan droops from her shoulders. Her cat jumps into each new coil of film that falls.

'So don't you want to talk about your problem?' she says without turning away from her pictures.

'I don't have one.'

'No? That's funny, because I think maybe you do.'

'_'

I stare at her red shoes side by side on the floor by the television, scuffy and in need of a clean. One is cracked from lace-eyes to hole. I estimate the length of the tear, hear Zoe's words and see the lips that form them but can't connect the two.

'Why do you drink so much?' she says.

'Because I want to.'

'What kind of answer is that? That's not an answer.'

'Of course it is. Why does everybody keep on at me about it? I do actually have a choice here, you know.'

'If you had a choice then you probably wouldn't.'

'That's not true.'

74

'So who is "everybody"?'

'Oh... you, Robin...'

'Lydia?'

'No, Lydia's pretty cool about it.'

'I thought she might be. Look, if you don't talk to me then I can't help you.'

'Maybe I don't need it.'

'Then what do you need? Because you definitely need something.'

'Maybe I don't want you to. Maybe I just want to be left alone.'

'Is that really what you want?'

'I don't know.'

'What is it? You can tell me. You can tell me anything.'

She turns to face me at last. As each word leaves her mouth it becomes a sound that floats in the air between us. I chew my nails until my fingers bleed. Accept each word because I know they have no consequence, know I'm just passing through them and they through me.

'I'm an adult,' I somehow say, 'I think I can be treated like one.'

They seem so absurd, these rambling noises that could easily have come from anywhere.

'Okay,' Zoe is saying, 'if that's how you feel then I really can't see the point. I love you but it's impossible.'

I just stare. Pace with hands loose in pockets. Stop. Rock on my heels.

'I've had enough of this,' Zoe says, gathers stray scraps of film from the floor and bundles them into another carrier bag. 'Remind me the stuff I've already looked at is in the blue bag. I'm going to bed.'

She leaves the room. The bags on the chair where she sat, her cat already eyeing them. I follow Zoe. In the bedroom she undresses and gets into bed. Her clothes make me cry because everything in her is in them. Cry because they give her shape and history, weight beyond the mass of me. I get into bed too, tuck my body around her but she falls asleep too soon. I kiss her shoulders and listen for rain. Her armpits flaked with deodorant. Can feel her alive, feel every slim sound she makes transmitted through her skin. My fingers trace her, pit by curve, as if the freckles on her body were symbols, held patterns and secret signs I couldn't read. She rolls over, faces me, eyelids drawn down, her hair tangling at the ends. She's just a shallow snore now but I stare in the hope of more. Her face blurs as if each second copied it over and over, gradually ghosting her out of existence.

Before Zoe was even a blip to me, before John Lennon songs made me cry and the periphery of sleep meant free; my father was working in New Zealand. He had a job that I could do and I was due to fly there for six months. I spent a last afternoon with Ridley. We sat in his flat talking, then walked along the banks of the Thames, river far and solid below us, Ridley laughing and spreading his arms like wings as I walked away. Then me at home packing, mostly clothes and CDs and my favourite books. Then Ailsa phoned.

'Ridley's dead,' she said.

'What happened?'

'I don't know.'

'What do you know?'

'He was walking home from seeing you and three guys tried to rob him, he ran I think and they chased him, they caught up with him so of course he tried to fight, you know what he's like...'

I met her later, standing under a sagging shop canopy with curtains of rain all around us, Ailsa all soaked clothes and tears of mascara.

'So stupid,' she said, 'so stupid...'

We went back to Ridley's house, her house, the room drawing in shadows as we hugged through to albums that were recorded before either of us were born, she said 'What are you going to do? You should still go,' but I knew I couldn't.

Morning finds Zoe before I can. After four or five hours of sleep she wakes up, pulls on a tee-shirt, looks at me as if she doesn't know what should be happening in her head.

'Do you want some tea?' she says.

'Please,' I mumble, more an idea than a sound. She wanders out to the kitchen. The air is grey and pasty in my mouth. I duck my head lower and pull the duvet over my face, lost a little more in sleep before Zoe returns with tea and two yoghurts and a carton of orange juice.

'What time is it?' I say, gulp down orange juice and pour another glass. Zoe sits on the bed spooning blueberry yoghurt into her mouth.

'It's eight,' she says, 'I have to go out soon. I'm meeting someone at half ten. This guy I met at my preview. He wants to see my portfolio. Says he might be able to get me some ad work.'

'That's good.'

'Yeah. You should get up soon, too.'

'Can't I stay here?'

'Don't you have to go to work?'

'Yeah, I guess.'

'Well then.'

'I can't go in.'

'Why?'

'I just can't.'

'Because you've got another hangover?'

'No.'

'Then why? You can at least tell me why.'

'_'

She tears a comb through her hair, curses the tangles.

'Please?' she says, 'not even for me?'

She sighs and turns away. Wrinkles her forehead then she looks like someone else, says 'Well if you can't do that for me, and if you can't even tell me why, can't even talk to me, then...'

'Then what?'

She stands by the door, her fingers drumming her thigh. Through the closed curtains I glimpse daylight. Zoe is history. Every breath she takes drains more oxygen out of here. Looking at her I can do nothing. I'm a container. I fill myself with everything around me, pull it inside. I don't exist in any sense.

'So are you going or not?' she says, stares at me for a very long time. In her eyes I become transparent. Her words and the mouth that forms them, her skin and her blood and her hair, pass through and out of me.

'I need to start getting ready,' she says.

The day spreads low under impotent clouds. I'm riding the train to meet Lydia. Buildings pulled past carriage windows. A storm sidling up from behind far towerblocks. Even birds seem reluctant to take to the sky. I didn't go in to work, left Zoe's, went home, phoned work and bleated sick, slept a handful of hours, then a beer to level me before calling Lydia. It's half six now or some shape hour; I'm on the better side of drunk and the world tingles with possibility. Time is cool fluid that runs in my veins with my blood and alcohol.

'I can't believe you split up with Zoe,' Lydia says, 'what happened?'

In the pub again. In this space sealed by plastic and wood and concrete and glass, this ordinary place. Pint glass in hand. My fingers encompass it flawlessly. Each mouthful I swallow blossoms inside me. Lydia sitting opposite me, our legs fold under the table so easily. The room swells out behind us. Table and chairs and people and chatter flash back every colour.

'Well we haven't actually split up. We've just... well, you know.'

'You mean she dumped you?'

'No, I don't mean she dumped me. I guess we both decided we needed to be apart for awhile. Sort out what we both wanted. You know, from the world and from each other and stuff.'

'Sounds to me like she dumped you. Every time I hear stuff like that, it's usually coming from the mouth of someone who's just been dumped.'

'No, it's just... I don't know. She thinks I drink too much.'

'Yeah, tell me about it. Chloe kept saying the same thing about me. But what can you do? We assure them it's not a problem, and here we are sitting in the pub and whining about them.'

'I miss her already.'

'So it's still open? Not all done and dusted and finished with for good?'

'Yeah.'

'That's good. For your sake, I mean, because I guess it's really what you want, whether you like it or not. It's always the same with relationships. I mean I've only got your side on this and figure you won't tell me the absolute truth anyway, even if you wanted to, nothing to do with you, nobody would, but...'

Her words dissolve to ether. She sniffs and itches her nose-ring, rubs knuckles in circles in the pits of her eyes. I must be starting to smell. I've been wearing these clothes for days. My body so sharp and out of focus and moving to imaginary music. I go to the toilet, sure I went there a few minutes before, nothing comes out, guess I must have done.

'You okay?' Lydia says when I get back to her.

'Yeah, yeah, I feel good, I'm just a bit tired,' don't want to talk about Zoe anymore and don't want to drift into Ridley. Sometimes we don't talk, just laugh and feather through each other, an affection that doesn't need language. Lavender scent like Ridley in the air around us. Lydia fingers a Coca Cola bottle left on the table, says 'I can't see the point of going to the pub and not drinking something alcoholic. It's like pulling someone and taking them home and not shagging them. I know people say it's sociable, but what kind of excuse is that?'

'_'

'So when are you and Zoe going to get back together?'

'I don't know. Most days I can't really get my head around

80

time.'

'Oh I know what you mean. I'm exactly the same. I can think in terms of what I'll do today, that's easy, tomorrow's a bit tricky but I can usually manage it, but two or three days from now is just impossible unless I've got something amazing lined up. But... yeah. Zoe. You seemed so good together, so happy, well I guess as happy as anyone can be tethered to just one other person, the world a lobster and all that, but... Well, I don't think it'll be too long before the two of you are touching toes again.'

I need to piss again, can't believe it. In the toilet the room is white tiles; I always sit now rather than stand, gives at least a hope of accurate aim. Back to Lydia. A sign above her head says

THIS IS NOT AN EXIT

'You didn't answer my question,' she says as I sit down.

'What was it?'

'I can't remember.'

I shrug, move to light a cigarette before realising I already have one burning down to my knuckles. Look at Lydia. The tip of her tongue poking out between her lips. In my head we go back to her flat and fall asleep fully clothed in each other's arms. Empty glasses on the table, see them all lined up, 'you just can't get the fucking service anymore,' Lydia says, gulps beer and it spills down her chin. I sort through the crumpled mess of money in my pocket, drop my empty glass on the table, say 'same?'

'No, I need to go really. I'm supposed to be meeting Chloe.'

'I thought you dumped her.'

'I did. I just fancy a shag and I can't be bothered to go out and pull.'

Going outside to nowhere. I cough to kick-start my lungs. My cigarettes can't quite find the pocket they belong to. Lydia moves to kiss me but misses, we laugh our way to the pavement and back up again.

'Call me soon,' she says, pulls her lapels around her, slopes towards a dotted line of taxis. I turn away from her, don't want to go home just yet. The wire skeletons of market stalls, a long walk to something that matters. The trick is to keep moving. Each step I take that lets ground gain on me. No matter which direction, I'm bound to hit a station some time. The stars get louder and louder. At the end of the street I turn back again. Where do I go? What do I do? Is there anything I should be doing? Somehow stepping through my door. Coats hanging in the hallway look like the shadows of strangers. I turn. The wall looms too close too soon and I'm mopping up a nosebleed with toilet tissue. The city beyond my window drowned out under piss-coloured rain. Lie on the bed, sniff out a cosy space, pull two pillows one large one small into my embrace and they make a Zoe-size shape. I float in a vacuum, happy now, numb and further than stars. I was never here. I have never existed. I was never born.

I wake up and my mouth has sealed over. Wipe a scum of mucous and saliva from my lips, smear it across my trousers. Sunlight fading behind the blind. The day was overcast, I think. I haven't left the flat for four days. Don't want to move but I know I'll have to soon. There's nothing left for me to put inside myself; just a loaf of moulding bread, a few potatoes, three cans of beer, a bottle of wine, half a pack of cigarettes, six inches of vodka.

Where is Zoe? I can't feel her. Has she even existed? I call but get her ansaphone, her voice as distant as another country's news. I reel in memories of her, write them down to give her form. Miss the way her body bends around my thread-worn sheets. Try for more Ridley memories too. Sometimes I still feel him here. His body the walls, the windows his eyes, his breath the air, his blood soaked up in the wine-stained carpet. The birds are singing in a place beyond these walls,

'the birds are singing,' Ridley says, 'it's night and blacker than black, but they're singing...'

and it doesn't seem odd that I haven't seen him for six months. If I had gone away I'd be getting back to him around now.

I fall asleep, awake at five, don't want to open my eyes. On the bathroom floor with a towel loose around my shoulders and a spilt beer can in my hand. Sick of waking up in a different room to the one I fell asleep in. Swallow some water from the tap. Don't really get hangovers any more. Go to the shop on the corner of the street for cigarettes, stop in the pub first. Stand against the bar, tear the plastic skin from a packet of vending machine cigarettes. A man asks me for a light then asks my name then asks who won the football. I shake my head and we chatter. He talks in sharpened points like Ridley used to, glares at me when I leave, don't remember what I said. Remember kicking the table and mumbling 'I don't want another fucking drink,' glasses everywhere and caught in a rain of ashes.

'What a fucking waste of good beer,' he says.

By the time I reach the street the shop on the corner has closed. The rain hangs in the air without going anywhere.

In my flat again, lying on the floor, alcohol a cosy brown blanket wrapping me. Empty vodka bottle poking out of the bin. My body all rusty red itches. Think I'll stay here until a better idea comes around. The TV radiates a methodical static light. Sleep so sore beneath my eyelids. I open the wine, determined to keep on drinking in the hope of where it might take me. Until I'm sick or pass out or die, or until the whole mess unveils itself to me. Lie on my back, rest the glass on my gut. Want to take the parameters of this world, turn them out of shape until they conform to me. Want to discard everything I can recognise even vaguely as human. Anything pulled in by the wake of history, the baggage of every year and of every idea. Become just light, a wave or particle impulse. Cigarette falling from my lips. Every match I strike is breaking. Can hear a noise like cicadas. The birds have run out of songs.

The world grows brighter at the edges of the windows. Silvery and liquid under my skin, getting hotter from the inside out, alcohol pushing through me. Everything converging at the solar plexus. I'm breathing out the reflected light of everything around me. Pushing out skin that doesn't matter, turning it into sound. I'm made of the light and the light is all there is. Dribbles of vomit trailing from my mouth, the world so white I close my eyes then black -

Ridley stands by the window, one hand holding the blind aside. He swings from side to side on his heels. Smiles. Eyes dark as oceans, stubble a sharkskin sheen. Words take form inside his mouth, flap from his tongue and through the air like birds.

'Let's go.'

He opens the window, wind turning his hair to cirrus clouds. I step up to the window-ledge, see cars and pavement and people below, scared but Ridley takes my hand and we

jump

glide   through

time-zones, release the earth and watch it turn below us. Chart rainstorms over Brazil and the spiral paths of islands across the Pacific Ocean. Antarctica gliding away from us in giant waves. Stars squint happy at us, My body getting softer, our hands joined in freefall as we mesh through each other. Thinning and out and soon we are transparent. Look at all the people sleeping below us, their minds rise through their upturned faces, we bid their mouths to open and we watch as they spiral up to join us. The city a black sprawl beneath, the sky a mess of stars in every direction, the mouth of history open. The sun burns out in another sky not ours -

Binary

When I was a child my pretended parents taught me how to see the stars. I preferred the sounds of the names to the stars themselves; Deneb, Altair, Capella, Aldebaran, words you could swill in your mouth, swallow and make a part of you.

Elsa is a photograph. Super eight of pale arms arcing across a dance floor as the Berlin Wall falls to dust. In a Hamburg hotel room we fuck on an aching mattress, the happy static of the television making it a threesome. Onscreen, ET is sodomising President Clinton. His phone-home finger glistens with ectoplasmic pre-come. He cycles to a world where greys caress under red skies circled by orgone bioforms, their translucent bodies shining within foreign suns. I like the television screen. It is mutable. Can contain me. Elsa's face bending out of shape until two teardrop-shaped eyes peer down at me as I lie on the receptacle of the bed. Our relationship is perfect. Her English almost as non-existent as my German.

Like oceans I convect into clouds, watch the grey stunted soil of Europe beneath me. My mother was a Pleiadian, my father a Draconian. I am the bastard child of star-crossed lovers. 'I was just there tonight,' Elsa says in her stuttering English. 'You would have gone with anyone.' I have learned to read her thoughts, to translate them into matter, to dip my Kirlian fingers inside her brainpan, let them merge with her cells, bristle through synapses and neurons. 'The English are such a guilty race,' she says, 'they are forever burdened by history, they can never accept that what is done is done and that they no longer need to worry for it.' And I know Elsa is right, that we can never understand ourselves until we learn to view ourselves as global.

Elsa has a car. We speed autobahn to autobahn, watch the sky turn black in the rear view mirror. The world shrinks to me, to Earth and Moon struggling within one orbit. As Elsa drives I sit beside her, rub my itch-red skin and wait for the buzz of another city on the horizon. Hanover, Dortmund, Essen, Dusseldorf, pass us in a concrete mess of light and dead skin cells. The smog and sunken rivers and bloated fish and squandered grass are new friends for us. Every tree we pass makes me want to soap and condition my hair until it reeks of forest fruits. Each realm, each shire we move though has hotels and beds and televisions. It's startling how long a relationship without words can continue. Our lack of language makes sex and empathy so easy; we can dispense with culture and conversation, focus on the proscribed incentive. I stare at the road until tarmac is my eyes. My axons dilated to the point of absolute elsewhere. Inside the meat of her car I feel at ease.

In a Cologne bar we are proffered bed-partners but know each offer is as stupid as coins, as money. Elsa is the chosen companion for me. We shake out of the clothes that contain us, push our bipedal mammalian bodies into shapes of pleasure. Want to fuck inside a crop circle. Want to mutate her flesh, resolve her into pixels until she is nothing but a digital image. I rise out of the trembling shell of me, look down at us. The human form is such a quaint and archaic design. Elsa stands in the doorway now; Bonn. One hand on either side of the frame, her body in the shape of a cross. She opens her mouth and speaks unfamiliar words. I meet her lips and they taste of ashes. When her mouth is all I can see she is perfect. We share cigarettes and I watch her fingers spider through the air between us. One eye open and one eye closed; her skin is sunyata. I wait for every hotel room to assume me. To deliquesce with my cells until Elsa and rooms and me are a single symbiotic organism.

The mothership is upon us. Art Bell taught me my true inheritance. Though Hale-Bopp skimmed our skies in a flash of neon and then passed on, I know my flesh will be vindicated. Some nights slender aliens graze my skin with white light, absorb me into the belly of their mothercraft and watch as I mate with their kind, their sallow heads bobbing with recognition. Lately I have been watching the stars again. If I watch a particular star for any period of time it swells out at me, picks on me, absorbs me. I add it to my repertoire of stars.

Disappear Here

Since I was brought to this room two days ago, the world has grown very quiet. Only slow voices and the scratch of pen on paper. Today as yesterday, a doctor with one enlarged left nostril sits by my bed and chain-sucks mints, writes down each word I say before weighing me.

'And what about dreams?' she says.

'What about dreams?'

'Are there any particular dreams you have that bother you? Any that stand out? Do you have any recurring dreams?'

'Yeah,' I smile, 'I have a recurring dream.'

'Do you want to tell me about it?'

'In my dream I'm all that exists, and the universe is expanding, every time I take a breath I expand until I can't expand any more, then I start to shrink into myself, until I disappear. Into my own black hole or something. The I explode and expand again. Endlessly, over and over, on and on with every breath. What do you think of that?'

'And how long have you been having that particular dream?'

'I don't remember.'

'Have you had it since you came here?'

'Yes.'

'I see you had some post this morning,' she says.

She lifts an envelope of papers from the table by the bed, fingers the first few sheets.

'Excuse me, that's private,' I say, and she puts it down. 'Was there anything else you wanted?'

'The nurse will be coming in shortly to take a blood sample. Please, try to co-operate with her this time.'

'You want my blood? Again? And you wonder why I look so pale.'

'It wouldn't kill you to at least try to eat something, either,' she smiles.

'You know what the problem is here?' I say. 'The problem is that you think there's something wrong with me. There isn't. I know exactly what I want. Now please, leave me alone so I can reach it.'

'So what do you want?'

'For now, or for the future?'

'For now?'

'For now... I want to move without making a sound. I want to live on nothing but air. I want to become my breath.'

'And for the future?'

'Another time. Work it out.'

By night I lie in the dark, spread myself as flat as I can be on the bed and listen to the sounds my body makes, a primeval hum accentuated by the rasp of air conditioning through a grate in the wall. Nine days ago my skin was itchy-red and scaly but now it's retreating, bluing out, nearing translucent, bones shining through like the columns of a submerged temple.

Eyes hovering at a locus between my head and the ceiling, I place my palms flat on my chest, count ribs beneath my fingers. Sometimes I can reach sleep like this, counting backwards bone by bone until I disappear down the rabbit hole of my navel.

Whoever thought that putting minds inside bodies was a good idea? All that eating and drinking and excreting and farting and belching and sex and bleeding and sleeping and dying.

My parents were here yesterday. When the nurse led them in I was sitting up in bed, pillows behind me underpinning my spine, wearing white hospital-issue clothes with the name printed on the back in watery blue.

'I thought you said this was all finished with,' my mother said, breaking up a plastic cup, drivels of coffee staining her clothes and fingers. 'And poor Hannah, she didn't know what to do. If she hadn't brought you here I don't know what we'd be doing. She said she thought you were doing it deliberately. She said she thought you were trying to kill yourself. I told her you weren't. You're not, are you?'

'I've never felt better.'

'But you're so...'

Her words resolved themselves into liquid which she swabbed

from her eyes with tissues.

'Look at you!' she says. 'The doctors said you could die.'

'The doctors don't know anything.'

'Of course they do,' my father says, turning the corners of a newspaper in solid fingers, 'that's why they're doctors and why you're here.'

'We brought you some clothes, too,' my mother says. 'Nobody wants to have to wear hospital clothes. Hannah sorted out some of yours, and there's some of your dad's there, too. I still can't understand it. You used to be so healthy when you were little. There was nothing you wouldn't eat.'

Yes. Me stood by the living room window, watching the day disintegrate under the weight of night. Father home from work by six. He trimmed rogue hairs from his ears and nostrils with nail-clippers, let his body sink roots into his chair, at perihelion to the television. My mother still in the kitchen. The beer can in my father's hand, the television, his chair, the plate on his lap, were a mass that swelled to engulf the space that surrounded him. On the other side of the room, away from his spillage, I sat pushing a loaded spoon into my mouth.

It's morning. I stare at the plate of food the nurse brought in for me. More like Caesar's feast than breaking fast. Two slices of toast, two tubs of margarine, a bowl of corn flakes and milk, a glass of orange juice and a glass of milk which I sniff then know is full-fat. I poke amongst the corn flakes, find one that hasn't yet liquefied. Turn it in the tips of my fingers, can't imagine it in my mouth, chewed by my teeth, slithering past my tongue, swallowed, ingested. I sip the orange juice twice, dribble one sip back into the glass. It's easier to eat nothing than to only eat a little.

I put the tray on the floor by the door, close the curtains. The nurses and doctor always open them when they enter the room, and I always close them when they leave. Back in bed I pick up the package I received in yesterday's post. An A4 envelope of photocopied sheets, and a covering letter.

...Hope the enc. are useful. Why do u want this stuff all of a sudden? You never seemed that interested before. Not sure what you're looking for, hope you'll find it here... Whatever. Anyway hope you're back w. reality soon. Steve.

I can't get comfortable. My pillows are solid blocks. The sheets scratch against the tips of my bones. I can feel that orange juice wriggling down my oesophagus like a tapeworm. I put the letter aside, look through the pages that accompanied it. Four chapters in all, headed The Nature Of Space And Time, Hertzprung-Russell Diagram And Main Sequence Stars, The Chandrasekhar Threshold - Neutron Stars And Black Holes, and Inside The Singularity. I turn the pages, read lines and paragraphs that catch my eye.

...In 1930, Subrahmanyan Chandrasekhar, an Indian student of Physics, calculated that if a moderately large star exhausts its hydrogen supply, and consequently begins gravitational collapse, it will continue to collapse without limit... It should be remembered here that when

matter is compacted into a smaller area it's mass and consequently it's gravitational attraction becomes greater... Even after having ejected most of it's mass... The star's enormous mass will cause it to shrink, getting smaller and smaller under the sheer weight if it's own gravity until it is literally crushed out of existence at a single point. During this implosion the gravity around the star becomes infinite, space and time fold in on themselves, and the star literally disappears from the universe. What is left is known by astronomers as a black hole.

It's so cold in here. I pull on a dressing gown my parents brought me; my Father's. The sleeves hang down to my knuckles. I can't decide if I need to go to the toilet. Have a feeling in the pit of me, as if something is curving sluggish through my bowels. Teasing. There can't be anything in there to come out.

I contract stomach-muscles, swing my legs to the floor, every atom of my body focused on exertion as I teeter to my feet. Walk through a corridor in my father's pyjamas and dressing gown. I can't move too fast without my body dizzying me. Pyjamas rolled up at wrists and ankles, my slippered feet silent on beige linoleum floor. I'm not supposed to go to the toilet or anywhere unchaperoned, partly because they think I can't make it that far and partly because they think I'll try to make myself sick. Not that much goes in or comes out of my body anymore. I'm a hollow, sealed at mouth and sphincter and urethra.

I sit on the toilet, elbows pressed into thigh-bones, shaking and shivering, but nothing happens. A sign by my head reads Pull Cord For Assistance. A string with an orange handle hangs from the ceiling. I hate this feeling. If there's waste to come out then let it flow, otherwise, body, leave me alone.

I flush and wash my hands. Take off dressing gown and pyjamas, stand in front of the mirror. A touch to my head leaves my fingers thick with flaky hairs. My body a savage geometry of drum-tight skin, limpid veins and jarring bones, covered in a silvery sheen of downy hairs. Limbs taut as rope. Brittle finger-nails. Scarred arms from my teenage hatings. Legs swelling a little at the ankles.

In the corridor back to my room I pause at a window, watch people pass through the quadrangle outside. Clouds hang in fleshy ribbons on the spine of morning. I'm glad Steve remembered to send me that material. A few months ago I was with him and Hannah, sitting on his sofa watching a television programme about star formation and black holes and warped spacetime. Steve quaffed beer, alternated talk and belches throughout adverts. Hannah's head rested on my shoulder, our bodies looped together at legs and arms. We haven't slept together for what I think are weeks but she insists are months. She wanted to be a model once, 'I want to be a big success in America,' she'd told me, as if there were eyes that cared to see, as if America were only California. Steve passed round biscuits and peanuts and crisps. I took a biscuit, put it in my mouth, wanted it to pass through without tainting me. Could feel the chocolate coating eat away at my teeth and gums, burrow past tongue to throat, sink into my stomach, planting seeds of fat. Could feel my body filling out, spreading under the futile touch of my fingers. Most people, I've noticed, can't watch television without simultaneously feeding.

A woman in a hospital gown and clutching a drip runs past me in the corridor, a nurse trailing behind her. They disappear through the swing doors leading to the toilet. Outside, people move from one side of the quadrangle to the other, wind pushing leaves ahead of them. How empty to have a purpose in life that extends beyond yourself. Where do they go? To their homes, to wards, to the cafeteria where they gather to feed. 'We're taught to swallow food like we're taught to swallow anything else,' a friend once told me, 'why else do you think it's called consumerism?' They think they have control of their lives but they don't. To have control you need to get inside, to the dark and hidden places where cells divide and multiply.

'It's fascinating,' Steve said, sucking the salt from each peanut before chewing it, 'I mean, how do you make sense of anything in a universe made of particles so small they're theoretical?' But for me, watching that television programme with him and Hannah let everything fall into focus. Then I knew exactly what I had to do. My days of a Mars bar or four pizzas or a quarter of an apple or twelve packets of crisps or nothing for lunch are over. No more eating then making myself sick, or hiding food so people think I've eaten it. All that seems so immature now. I'm on another plateau.

'What are you doing out of bed?'

I turn to see a nurse striding towards me.

'Come along,' she says, 'let's get you back to your room.'

With fingers like tweezers on my scant arm she leads me down the corridor. With every movement my bones shift, rubbing together at the joints like tectonic plates. In my room she puts me to bed, tucks harsh sheets around me.

'You didn't eat your breakfast,' she sighs. 'You know the only

96

way we can get you better is for you to start eating again. And what's it doing on the floor?'

I don't answer, don't look at her. She picks up the tray, puts it on the table by the bed.

'I'm going to have to sit here until you eat it,' she says, and sits down.

'I can't eat that, not with you sitting there staring at me.'

'I won't stare. I'll just mind my own business until you've finished.'

I can't eat it, anyway. I'll be sick.'

'If you don't want that then we can fix up something else for you. I'll drop you in a menu later. What do you fancy?'

'Nothing. Oxygen. If you're so keen to feed something then feed yourself, your children, anybody, just leave me alone.'

'But aren't you hungry?' she says.

'No. I don't get hungry any more. Hunger is a construct.'

'Don't be silly,' she says. 'Now you're just being silly. Come on, just some cereal. How about some cereal? It's good for you.'

'You can't force me to eat.'

'Of course they can. But they'd really much rather not have to do that. Come on. Not even a piece of toast? You must like toast. My little boy likes toast, and he doesn't like anything.'

'Plants have got the right idea,' I say, as she opens the curtains. 'They don't need to feed. They take in everything they need from the soil and the sun and the air.'

'Do you want to be a plant?'

'Now you're just trying to put ideas into my head.'

Curioser and curiouser. I don't really sleep any more. Prefer to lie awake through the night. In the dark the world seems far away. The light that pokes under my door, the goadings of food and the chatter of nurses at the end of the corridor, can't reach me. Alone I despond for the swell of skin cells, of finger-nails and hair. The doctor said they're no longer growing, 'not in your condition', but I know they are. Anything will replicate for its own sake for as long as it can.

I don't know whether I'm awake or asleep. Lose any sense of fast and slow until the tick of the clock in the corridor changes tone, denoting a change of hour. Inbetween, all is molten, timeless. When you suspend the needs of senses and body you realise that time is elastic.

Sometimes the idea of hunger is still inside me. This evening I ate an entire half an orange. I need to be more disciplined. Hunger is purely a weakness of the will. I know what I need to do. Telescope my body, strip it of all its functions. Motion and density are the only things that are real. Everything else is excess. The purpose is to shed mass, to compact myself as tight as possible, until not even light can penetrate or escape me. Work and lovers and friends and family are all layers to be expelled as I shrink to infinite density. Some nights between sleep and waking I can feel myself pulled through vacant space, receding further and further away and ever closer.

I wake up and don't want to do anything. Pillow wet with sweat and spilled saliva. Sunlight brims through the window. Somebody has brought in food and more post and a fresh jug of water. I remember the nurse saying, 'wake up, it's lunch time,' but I was still tied to sleep.

What happened to morning and to breakfast? Has the doctor been in yet? I don't know.

I look at the tray on the table. A plate, and a glass of milk. Full-fat again. On the plate, five brown slices of dead quadruped cohabit a slurry of congealing gravy with diced carrots, green beans, and boiled potatoes. I didn't order this. When the nurse gave me the menu card yesterday, I ticked the box marked Salad, having first crossed that word out and written Celery beside it. A friend once told me that she considered celery to be the perfect food, 'you use up more calories eating it than it gives you.'

I drink a glass of water, close the curtains, take the envelope from the tray. White and square and addressed in Hannah's scrawl. I open it. Can hear Hannah, squeaking every word as I read it.

...There are so many things I remember. Do you remember when I surprised you, we went for a picnic by the river? You hardly ate a thing, you told me you'd had lunch with Steve earlier. I was talking to him later and he told me it wasn't true. You didn't have to lie to me. All you had to do was talk to me. I think of all these things and it makes me cry... I know now why we haven't made love for so long. Is it because you didn't want me to see you? Didn't want me to see what you were doing to yourself? But I knew. I always knew. I could tell just by holding you. Not even that, just by looking... So much was unspoken between us, but I know exactly how you feel. I know you won't believe me, but I understand what you're going through. I know it's hard, but you can

overcome this. Please trust me. I'm crying as I write this. Please get better soon. I miss you.

I fold the letter in half, write 'If it wasn't for you I wouldn't be here' on it, return it to the envelope, write Return To Sender on the back, slot it between milk glass and plate on the tray for the nurse to take away. Open the cabinet by the bedside, take out the information Steve sent to me.

...It is difficult to explain the topology of black holes in sensical language. The most common kind of black hole, the Schwartzschild or non-rotating black hole... consists of an event horizon surrounding a singularity. The event horizon is the 'outer edge' of the 'hole', the point at which spacetime is infinitely warped, allowing nothing - not even light - to escape. 'Within' the back hole lies the singularity, the point of infinite density into which the star itself has collapsed... The chief problem with singularities is that they render all our notions of understanding, all our physics and our mathematics, redundant...

I hear the tuning of the door handle, return the papers to the cabinet. The doctor comes in, clipboard and a green card wallet folder under her arm.

'Good afternoon!' she says. 'And how are we today?

'I feel fine. I don't know about you, though.'

'You haven't eaten your lunch yet.'

100

'What did you expect?'

'This isn't doing you any good at all.'

'But don't you see? My body's tuned differently to yours. I've deliberately programmed it that way. By giving me food you're killing me.'

'Look... I don't think you realise the gravity of your position. You simply can't carry on like this. All we want to do is help you. We just want to make you better.'

'You mean, make me like you.'

'No, that isn't what I meant.'

I turn away from her.

'Did you want anything else?' I say.

'Just a little talk, that's all.'

'What's the point of that? You don't listen to anything I tell you, anyway.'

'Of course I do.'

'It won't make any difference.'

'I'd just like to chat with you about a few things, that's all.'

'Like what?'

'Let's get some light in here first.'

She walks over to the curtains and opens them. Through the window, trees are flesh-stripped skeletons dotted with meagre leaves.

'Your mother called earlier,' she says, 'to see how you were doing.'

'And what did you tell her?'

'We told her the truth, that there was no change yet. She sends her love. How do you feel about your parents?'

'How do you mean?'

'Well... would you say that you were close? They seem to really worry about you.'

'That's because they're parents. It's what parents do. I don't particularly care about them either way. They're just there, that's all.'

'Would you say your childhood was a happy one?'

'I guess.'

'What about dinner? Did you usually all eat together?'

'You're not being very subtle at all. Yes, we all ate together. No, I don't think they over-fed me, no more than any parent would. No, they didn't deprive me of affection, smother me, or abuse me. You really don't get it, do you?'

'Get what?'

'Never mind.'

'No, tell me. I'd like to know.'

'It's not important.'

'Of course it is. Of course you're important.'

'I know- oh, forget it.'

I stare at my fingers then back at her. She squints myopic at the clipboard in her pale and foamy hands.

'What was school like?' she says.

'Normal,' I yawn. 'What about you?'

'What do you mean?'

'Well how about if I ask you the questions for a while?'

'But that's not what we're here for. We're here to help you.'

'Don't you think you need helping, then?'

'That's not the point.'

'You can at least tell me what your school was like,' I say. 'If you expect me to answer your questions, you can at least tell me that.

Trust is a two-way thing.'

She sighs and grinds her teeth. Must be out of mints.

'Well... okay', she says. 'I went to a Grammar School, all girls. I lost touch with most of them as soon as I went to Medical College. We used to have a class reunion every year. I haven't been to one for a good while now. I just haven't had the time. They send round a newsletter every few months. Usually it's full of obituaries. You still haven't told me what it is you want for the future.'

'To attain the perfect body-weight.'

'I can understand that,' she says. 'All anorexics have a weight goal. But you have to realise that-'

'Pardon?'

'I mean, it's understandable for you to have that feeling. All anorexics-'

'I'm not anorexic.'

'Recognising it is often the most challenging phase.'

'It's not a phase.'

'So what would you say your ideal weight is?'

'Zero.'

'Zero isn't a very realistic target.'

'Okay, then, four stone seven pounds.'

'But you must realise-'

'Yes. At that weight the body can no longer function. Can no linger support it's own mass. That's the intention.'

'Then you'll die.'

'No I won't.'

'I see you also have a history of bulimic activity,' she says, flicking through the papers on her clip-board.

'If that's what you'd choose to call it.'

'What would you prefer we called it?'

'It's not such a peculiar thing. I mean, cats eat grass to make themselves regurgitate any unwelcome visitors to their stomachs.'

'It's not quite the same, though, is it? And now with your refusal to eat-'

'Eskimo shamen believe that fasting is the best way to obtain knowledge of all the hidden secrets of nature. Did you know that? Christ spent forty days and forty nights in the wilderness. Moses fasted on Mount Sinai...'

'Yes, but what could you possibly need to know so badly? What are you trying to avoid? And in your condition...'

'And what would you say my condition was?'

'Unless you start eating very very soon, you're going to die. Do you know what hyperalimentation is?'

'I've heard of it.'

'So you know what it involves?'

'Remind me.'

'We give you a local anaesthetic,' she says, 'then we attach a catheter to a vein just under your collar-bone, the subclavian vein, right above where your heart is, so we can feed a nutrient solution direct into your body. It's mainly fats, amino acids, vitamins, minerals, dextrose... Don't worry, it won't hurt at all.' She pauses. 'We follow this up with a combination of liquid diet and proper food, up to around 3,000 calories per day. The aim is to get you to gain, say, one to three pounds per week.'

'No. No way.'

'We might not be in the position to choose.'

'I'll discharge myself.'

'I don't think that would be a very wise idea. If you do that, and if you continue the way you have been, you're going to die.'

I have divided my life into two pieces; before I was brought to this room, and after. I'm glad I came here. Before, there were too many distractions. This room gives me space away from everything, time to accomplish what I know needs to be done. As soon as you remove the tethers of eating, the world glows with a soft fuzz of perfect clarity. You can feel the geometry of your body warping the space around it, mind in equilibrium, your senses humming so alive to everything. Can see the atoms bound up in the paint on the walls, or the hairs on the legs of the fly that circumnavigates the lampshade above you. Can smell the sweat of the snorer in the room next door. Can hear the motion of your skin. Can still taste that glass of water now seeping through you. Everything does itself for you. All time envelops you, past and present and future and timeless, charged and pulsing and meaningless.

I lie in my bed uncertain of the points that define waking and sleeping, that separate object from object. It feels like almost dawn. The room is organic, a warm Pre-Cambrian ocean into which my body diffuses, until I can't distinguish the walls of the room from the floor from the ceiling from the bed or from my body. Approaching the singularity of four stone seven pounds. The world pulling in, tighter and tighter, until the room is all there is and there can be no outside because nothing else exists. My body unseaming cell by cell, fading to the naked bones and my bluest of veins, merging until there is no distinction between body and mind and me, until there is only infinite curved space.

Citizen

Two years ago. Father's fingernails dug into the soiled mattress. Hair flaking to the pillow, skin wrinkled as old dollar bills. My fingerprints on the mirror that he mists with his rotten-tooth breath. Pistols hang in dusty cases over the bed. I pace the room drinking Coca Cola, can after can, leave their crushed shells piled around him. He would never let me drink coke when I was a child.

Sat in the corner while he sleeps, turning the pages of paperbacks, not really reading them, just touching the pages and liking the feel of a book in my hands. I rest my book on the arm of the chair, peel an orange with my favourite knife. Juice slips under my chewed back nails and stings. A single unbroken spiral of orange skin hangs from my fingers. I eat each orange segment slowly.

Stand, knife in hand, bang the blade against the metal frame of the bed; it clangs like fencing foils, and father's eye loll open.

I stoop, hold the knife behind my back, run my fingers along its edge. It needs sharpening.

'I want you to die young, die soon...' he smiles. 'So I can... outlive you... I want you to die young...'

I turn away.

'Can you change the sheets?' he says.

I nod; he mutters back to sleep, a sputter of phlegm and syllables, and I know the sheets can wait. Hold the mirror to his mouth again. It still clouds over.

Sitting, listening to the rush of his snoring, swinging the chair on its back legs, rocking to the rhythm of my lungs filling then emptying with Marlboro smoke. Old Pink Floyd lyrics in my head. The book falls to the floor. I drop my Marlboro butts and empty cartons onto the carpet with the book and coke cans. Drum my fingers. The room reeks of his sweat. I want to breathe in his air, foul it with nicotine, use it all up and choke him.

'Excuse me. You dropped these.'

She stops, turns, swings on the heels of her calf-high boots. I hold out the bundle of keys I watched tumble from her pocket.

'Excuse me, you dropped these.'

She walks towards me, smiles, takes the keys from my hand.

'Thanks,' she says.

'No problem.'

'She tucks the keys back into her pocket.

'Thanks,' she says, walks away. I follow; five paving slabs and I'm beside her.

'What's your name?' I ask.

'Why?'

'Just curious.'

'Well don't be.'

She stops, looks at her reflection in the window of a pasta restaurant. Rain specks her turquoise PVC coat.

'You're very rude...' I sigh.

'Yeah?' She starts walking again.

'Yeah. If it wasn't for me, you'd have got home and wouldn't have been able to get in.'

'I'd have broken a window. Or stayed with my boyfriend.'

She stops by the roadside on the corner of Bloomsbury and New Oxford Street, puts out her arm and a taxi glides to the kerb.

'I only wanted to know your name...' I say.

'Knightsbridge,' she says to the driver and opens the door.

I wash my hands.

I like power because it thrills me. Because it surges with the blood that fills the veins. Because the veins pulse and bulge on the side of the head. Because brilliant white light burns inside the brain and ignites fires in all your cities.

I live alone with five kittens. Stand high in the lounge; tiny room. Meagre chairs and pot plants. Yesterday's magazines. My hands on the stereo speaker.

I move in giant steps from corner to corner. Cat piss and worms of shit, sandalwood perfume oil. First the fingers then the toes. First the eyes and then the ears. Sweat runs down the arms, slick and tasting sweet. Shirt clings to the body. I pull it off, free the sweat, revel inside the skin.

King of all I see.

A kitten waddles out across my path. Stops and stares up at me. I was born to be looked at.

I have favourite kittens. One a gorgeous flame-coloured tabby, the other completely black except for a white stripe down its face. I have named them Flame and Stripe. The other kittens have few distinguishing features and don't deserve names.

I move from room to room, wearing only torn jeans. Each step is an exercise in precision. Stand by the window, watch the people in the street. Time is slurred. The sun sets outside but it must be morning. Taste of a day's Wild Turkey.

In the bathroom. Touch the face in the mirror, curve lips, push fingers in. Melting. Touch the face. Shave Taste foam and soapy water on lips. Seeds of blood. Remove jeans. Masturbate at the mouth in the mirror.

In the bedroom I choose clothes for the evening. Angel rainments that let me shine. Take down a charcoal grey suit and black shirt. Dress in front of the mirror, excitement swelling like beaten skin. Pause every few seconds, savour each new configuration of cloth on pink flesh.

Love the image in the mirror. Can do anything when I am adored. Can stop the earth in spinning. Can turn the seasons round. Summer-hot December.

Apart from Flame and Stripe, all the kittens run when I enter the lounge. I grab one as it is disappearing behind a bookcase choked with videos. Black and white ankle-socks. Hold it inches from the face. Its mouth opens and closes as it mews; mechanical movement. Claws scratch the skin. Clench the fist. Kitten squeaks. I kiss its head, drop it and it scurries away.

In the hall I put on tall shoes, inch-high heels to lift me over everything. Leave the house and the gate squeals shut. Feet on pavement. Cracked slabs clumsily aligned. Mangled Coke cans. Pizza and wet earth smells. World in my hands.

When I wake I light a Marlboro. Smoke it to the end. Stub out, wait two minutes before lighting the next. It usually take four or five cigarettes before I can face the day.

'Steve?' I croak into the phone. 'I'm not coming in today. I've just woken up and feel like shit. Maybe I've got flu coming on or something.'

'Or maybe you've just got a hangover.'

'Bollocks.'

'You in tomorrow?'

'Maybe. I'll call you in the morning. I expect I will be. You know how much I miss you all.'

'Sure. Bollocks to you. Bye.'

I spend the day at home surrounded by screwed up Marlboro packets, crushed Budweiser cans, cracked window papered over and nailed shut. Shapes of clothing. Coins and crumpled banknotes. The walls of the hall are papered with ten and twenty and fifty pound notes.

I steer clear of the lounge, frightened by the mess I'm sure I've left there. Need something to eat first. Need a drink.

Friday today. I ride to work. Get off the tube at Victoria, pause at the park for a Marlboro and some clear air. A homeless guy in a red kagool and New York Yankees baseball cap slouches up to me. I turn away. He holds out a cigarette butt.

'Got a light?'

I proffer my Marlboro. It's always been Marlboros, even at fourteen. I admire myself when I can attain that simple strain of purity.

'You're a bit shaky,' he says, squints and lights his fag-end, holds up his trembling free hand.

'First cigarette of the day,' I lie.

'Yeah. Shakes. I get them too.'

I watch him walk away. Callused heels hang through the backs of his shoes. I love the city when the sun shines and lights up the fumes.

I leave the park and follow the spoor of money - past the Shakespeare Tavern and Bureau de Change, American Steak House Scotch Steak House Garners Big Uns Sutton Pawn Brokers don't push me Pizza Pizza Prima Pasta Abbey National Burger King Highland Steak House empty black-windowed watch them miss the bus watch them fall cross over Duke of York walk wait then walk; my costume for work is grey suit, white shirt, black shoes, grey tie. Always a uniform when I serve the city.

My first duty when I arrive at work is to collect the post from the security guard at reception, a sprawling African with a face like a scrotum. He sits beneath a silver plaque that reads MERCER THOMAS MERCER.

'Any post for me today?' I ask.

He just growls.

'Is this it?' I poke through a sack of letters on the floor by his desk. He rumbles again, turns away.

'Thank you,' I say, lug the sack downstairs to the post room. The sack is heavier than my father.

There are three of us in the post room. Jordan is a goateed American, skin the colour of blood, an ex-helicopter pilot who got shot down over Na Trang. Kath is twenty-six, same as me, lives with her boyfriend over a kebab shop on Queensway.

My second duty is to empty the post sack, sort the mail and then distribute it through the building one floor and department at a time. This usually takes most of the morning. The second post comes in at eleven. I don't know what Jordan and Kath do, exactly, never really look. Kath franks, licks stamps, folds letters, calls couriers. Jordan reads bristling Russian novels.

'How are you today, sir?' Jordan asks. Everybody is 'sir' to Jordan.

'Today I'm okay.'

'Are you? Good. Not many people can say that.'

He sets a Dostoevsky down. Pages spread like limbs. The table he sits at is strewn with biros and Post-Its and ripped crisp packets.

Sound of stirring tea. Facsimile bleeps. I hate the song the radio plays, hum along regardless.

'I'm sure the guy in reception doesn't like me,' I say.

'Who?'

'Don't know his name. The usual guy. Always. He's there every day. Don't know his name.'

'Why do you think he doesn't like you?'

'I just don't. I get that feeling. Maybe. I don't know. Ask him. I don't even know his name.'

'Does that bother you, not knowing his name?'

'No.'

'Never told you his name,' Jordan smiles. 'Let me tell you something. Know a person's name and you have the key to their soul.'

Dark, walking to the Shakespeare Tavern, agreed to meet Steve from MTM there. A guy sits on a rubbish bin down the side of Burger King. Slips a needle into his arm, pulls the tourniquet, slops his head back, happy; I smile, say 'don't worry.'

A page from my father's journal:

11 Nov - 11.45 zcc.s ace. No resp. AF. Snoring. 12.30 AF 2cc.s chlor.

12 Nov - 6.00 CR. Still fighting. 6.15 1.5 cc.s PH. 12.30pm AF. No reaction. 1.30 AF. Some vocal. 135 C and W. FFF.

13 Nov - First penis then enema. Slight resp. 2.00 phot overhead. 11.15-12.30 FF CF FF.

Sunday morning. Sun on bleary windowpanes. My flat smells. Everything is the same when I'm not working. Flicking through TV channels, watching the kittens playing on my floor, turning Marlboro butts in my fingers, working through a pack of Budweiser. King of

Beers. One wall of the room is covered, floor to ceiling, with video cassettes. Beside this is a slim case of paperbacks I stole from my father. On TV there's a programme about spiders in Finland. My kittens attack the empty cans I drop. Run through the hall, picking at the bank notes pasted to the walls. I don't remember how many kittens I've got, five or something. I like the idea of having kittens around.

'You should stop smoking.'

She doesn't answer, takes another drag. The smoke quickens my nostrils.

'It'll kill you.'

'You think I've never heard that before?' she says.

She looks away, puts her Evening Standard down on the bench beside her, opens a Diet Sunkist. She's mid-twenties, puffy body, occasional freckles, fingernails bitten away.

'No,' I say, 'I expect you've heard it a thousand times.'

'So why are you boring me with it?'

She picks up her paper, turns pages, smiles at Garfield, looks at the horroscopes. I light a Marlboro.

'Can't always get what you want,' I say.

Mother did not exist, only the shallow-breasted womb that birthed me, the hollow that shat me at the world. The hole Father used to get me here. I didn't have a Mother.

Father was the perfect misogynist.

Loomed high for as long as I can remember, even when I was still cot-bound, his baby-big hands bruising Mother's skin all day, each day, every day, and sometimes me. Me his only creation, the only part of the world he could call his own.

I spent my childhood days alone, friends not allowed into his house, me never allowed to visit theirs. Created worlds to be away from him, from anything. His house, big house, big walls, my room the tiniest, Mother always in the kitchen clearing up the messes he'd made. Always a 4-pack in the fridge.

When I was four years old he threw me down the stairs because I left some toys in a wrong room, dared play under his feet when he wanted to read his Financial Times. Picked myself up, face a bruised mess seeping blood, banister higher than me; he said, 'If you can stand up that easily then it obviously didn't hurt,' dragged me to the top and pushed me down again. Then again, again, until he was certain that pain had taught me.

He never took me places; my school friends went to football matches with their fathers, movies, the zoo, Macdonald's. When I was eleven he took Mother and me to the fair, dragged me by the hair all evening, wouldn't let me go on rides. So I sat on the ground by the waltzers, sucked candyfloss and watched kids zoom round rides with their fathers.

He had an edifice of porn magazines under his bed. Summer nights he'd lie on the bed and read them, sheet turned back, penis hanging out of his blue striped pyjamas, Mother sat on the bed beside him sometimes, make-up covering her split face, the pages of Woman's Own turned by her bloated fingers. On afternoons when he was at work and I was off school, I'd sneak into his room and pull the magazines out from under his bed, flick terrified through them, *masturbate; I couldn't imagine coming in the presence of a woman that actually moved.*

Monday to Friday beautiful. Nine in the morning until five thirty in the evening.

Pushing the mail trolley through the Seventh Floor, smooth sometimes scuffing on wires, I drop letters and parcels onto desks and into in-trays. Past Stephanie, new, tiny and big on curl.

'Here's your post, Miss Russell,' I say, dropping letters and a swollen Manila A4 onto her desk.

'Not there, please,' she says. 'In the tray. And the stuff that's in the tray already, that can go. So can you.'

She doesn't look up as she speaks. Doesn't meet my eyes. Fresh paper to busy her. Clean and shiny as new knives. I pick up the stack of letters in her tray.

To another desk, then another, another. Letters in and out again. Seamless. My life is so much easier when I tell myself how not to think. Love working. Live for those hours. Expand them inside me. Feed on the money and the faces I make, photosynthesis through pockets to skin or retinas to brain. Working I am cleansed, can like me. The second post comes in by eleven.

'Listen, we need a favour from you,' Steve says, an indigo-suited babytooth thing that lords my department with fingers in braces like holsters. 'You'd really be helping out. Juliette on phones has had to go to hospital, the guy she lives with was in an accident. Can you man the phones for her this afternoon? It'll be okay. Only first floor.'

'Sure. No problem. I'd enjoy the change. Sure. What did he

do?'

Fuck you Juliette. Fuck your desk, your four-tier in-trays, your telephone that rings, your Snoopy doll. Don't spill your offal on me. Not my job. Not my money. I have to sit here so you can go and see your boyfriend, the guy that you fuck, don't fuck each other, wouldn't know where to start, you have to go because he sliced off two fingers in the salt beef cutter? Who cares, he should expect it working in a restaurant, occupational hazard. Why do you have to be there? What are you going to do? Sew them back on? Suck the stumps? Medicinal blow-job? When your phone rings I'll slam it down. Cover your Post-Its with scrawl and pornography. Fill your drawers with Malrboro ash. Leave your Tipp-Ex bottles out to dry. Stand with the sun that's high outside. Sometimes I'm your father. Just want easy. Go tell some cunt that cares. I don't want to hear it. It's nothing personal. I just haven't got the time.

Stepping over low damp bodies in doorways. Most of the homeless around here know me well enough not to ask for cigarettes or for change. I walk up to the Thresher on Victoria Street for Bud and Wild Turkey. Over puddles under umbrella. A naked man stands on the corner of Vauxhall Bridge Road, directing traffic.

FATHER'S JOURNAL # 2
The first crucial requirement is the total cessation of subjective

thought. This is a far easier task than common opinion may portray it to be. It is a lie to think that human personality does not change and cannot be changed. The outer ego is changed constantly by events that occur in the world around it, by what is fed in by the senses and their consequent reactions. The inner personality - I guess the soul as some people will insist on calling it - can also be changed by direct outer methods. Brainwashing and sensory deprivation techniques prove that this is possible, that you can take what personality already exists and substitute it for something entirely different. The parent of course has a head start in a sense, since it has been proven that the bulk of the experiences that determine adult behaviour occur before the person has reached six years of age. What is personality, after all, but an interchangeable mask?

I wash my hands.

I've decided to make a list, The Ten Qualities In Myself Which I Most Admire.

1. Despite my childhood difficulties and the knowledge of all the things he did I have still become my own person.

2. I have a job and I have money.

3. I am attuned to the world around me. I know what I want in any given situation.

4. My friends respect my opinions. They listen.

5. My drinking can be a problem but I know how to rule it and not vice versa.

6. I know the city better than anyone I know.

7. None of them suffered unduly.

I'll finish this list later. First I'm rewarding myself with a Marlboro break.

A box filled with artefacts. It lives under my bed, reproduces when I'm not looking.

A passport, Ratners necklace, knot of keys, mangled Diet Pepsi can, spineless Milan Kundera novel, bottle of blue pills, biro, Madonna cassette with the tape spooled out, assorted rings, a tampon, nail file, a scrap of paper riddled with unintelligible scribble, twelve pesetas, twenty-eight francs, seven dollars forty-eight cents, a paisley sock, two paper clips, a travelcard dated 29th August last year, a lighter, bent-framed spectacles, a plectrum, an unwritten Picasso postcard, hair-brush, powder puff, finger nail, eraser, pair of swimming goggles, pet nametag saying SPOOK and a phone number, a book of matches, pink toothbrush, blood-stained scarf, Michael Jackson ticket stub, library card, address book, eye liner, pocket scissors, bank notes totalling twenty-three pounds and thirty-two pence. Owner skin all ribboned by time and by me, the box that stays to tell me what I've done.

I went to school between the ages of ten and thirteen. Father drove me there and home every day, taught me how to best hate women.

'The perfect woman is totally controlled,' he says, meeting my eyes in the rear view mirror. 'A woman who does exactly what she's told and nothing else. There are never any problems with a totally

submissive woman. There can be no problems, only pleasure and fulfilment.'

I curl the pages of exercise books around my fingers, swallow; my perception of hate is lopsided at best. I look away from him, follow the road, that same route every day. Over the rubbish-soaked Thames and past a wasteland pinioned by the A102 and factories that stank like the dinners mother burnt, sprawling with the piled-up corpses of cars, eight or nine deep, thousands, shattered windscreens and twisted frames rust-bloodied and mangled into new forms; the perfect signature for the world I know.

The history of my family is a history of money, more money than you can imagine, a trail of bank-notes and gold to be followed from past and out into future.

I sit staring at the television screen. Television was my third parent. My body drowned in sweat. I wear jeans and a tatty Pink Floyd tee-shirt. Kittens climb on me. I sit by the open fridge sometimes, drink Coca Cola filled with ice. All windows open. Shrieks of cars and people and TV. I always have the television on, even when I'm not at home. I hold my hands against the screen, static palms, mould my skin around it. Push my face in. On the news a plane has crashed in the Philippines, with over two hundred dead. Still sea, splinters of plane on the surface. Yellow inflatable boats between them. Helicopters overhead.

Father collects guns. Keeps them in a rack in his study and in a case above his bed. Three rifles and five pistols. Each morning after shaving - and he always shaves at 6.30, summer or winter - he takes them out, cleans them, postures in half-light, cocked, places them next to one another on his desk. Loose body in combat fatigues. Blows his nose. Places them one at a time back into the cases, locks the cases, takes the key with him when he goes to work.

His guns are like his porn mags. When he's out I sneak into his room, stare at the guns behind locked glass. One day - I guess I'm about thirteen - he's out and the case key sits in the lock. I turn it, take out a Bulldog .44, hold it, cold and heavy, a dead weight; spin circles around the room, squinting, pointing at imaginary fathers and shouting 'bang!'. Stop cross-legged on the floor. Two clicks. The first me, cocking the trigger and sensing a bullet in the chamber; it breathes there, like an unborn child inside a patient mother. The second click the door, shutting behind my father.

'You want to play guns?' he says. 'Give it to me.'

Terror makes me obey. He sniffs, coughs, spins the chamber and counts the bullets.

'Two out of six. Now I'll show you how we play with guns.'

He spins the chamber again, holds the gun against my temple, says 'move and I'll kill you.' Then mother in the doorway, running at him, him turning and pointing the gun at her, she running anyway, her hands white-knuckled on his arm; he tosses her aside, takes one of her hands, snap snap snap snap as he jerks her fingers back.

'Your mother is a waste of time,' he sighs, disenchanted now, pulls the trigger against my head.

A slide of movement in the brain sends me from one side of the room to the other.

She's walking through rain. Her shoes are shiny. Her umbrella joins the march of black toadstools.

I can see her through the window. I remove big hands from pockets. Turn away. A black bag hangs on the back of the door.

Time enough.

Work to be done.

Waiting.

The beginning of me was the beginning of the world. I was their third child, first born alive, forecep delivery, three weeks overdue. Mother screaming for me to die and Caesarean scalpels waiting. Father pacing the room next door and waiting for the midwife to be done. From the womb and delivered straight to his hands; he carried me, still bloody, to his study. Stalked euphoric, ignored my cries.

I replicate the facts as I can. Know the details because I found and read his journals much later. Born underweight and crying and vomiting. Three and falling down concrete steps, smashing my head then comatose for hours. Father.

Most of my childhood was a blot, a blind vacancy in which I distinguished nothing. Father's shadow always on the wall, him and banister cast like Nosferatu. Me curled up in a tree at the heel of the garden. Sallow green world away from him. In my room every morning before he left for work, pulling me from soaky bedcovers. Every time I wet the bed - and I did frequently, too scared to get up in the night – he'd hang the soiled sheets from the window. Sometimes hung me out there too, his thick fingers round my ankles, the world outside ready to show me humility, new piss trickling down my shaky legs. 'I want to make you perfect,' he says. 'I want to make you all the things I could never be. The first totally pure thing. Don't cry! Don't you dare cry at me!' I soon learned that the only way to stop him hitting me was to cease my tears. 'I never want to see you crying again. Ever.' And I watched from my window every day as he owned down the street to work, suited and with briefcase in his solid hands. By day I hid in my room, sometimes crept downstairs to watch with mother; cartoons and gameshows, Pebble Mill and sitcoms, she deflated on the sofa. Otherwise I sat in my room by the window, smeared fingerprints staining glass. You could hold a football match in our garden.

Father's voice was like his money.

'You don't need school,' he said. 'School would corrupt and pollute and destroy you. We need to keep you pure. You're destined for great things. Beautiful things. I'll never send you to school. Never let the crowd taint you. You belong to me, not them.' That pleased me. Then I knew he meant to make me something. Knew that I would be unique. Home every evening at 5:45, he changed from suit to combat fatigues. Once a month he stood me against the wall and charted my growth, tapped new data into his computer. And I believed all his words then, felt sure he did too, that his method could make me gold.

'Don't be afraid of money. Money isn't a thing to be ashamed of. You can trust money. Money is your friend. It can mean power, but power is also inside. In this world you need strength. Fearless. Guilt is the enemy you need to overcome. Kill guilt. Kill fear. Everything you defeat will push you further.'

So it was me, soft thing, until 'you've not grown much this

124

month,' and he slapped me. 'I beat you to make you strong. Don't take it personally.' Mother sat in front of the television, nodding along to the canned laughter. Awake at night, I heard his voice put out on her. Always felt safe then, knew there were at least two rooms between them and me. She didn't shout up anymore, even through his making me watch their fucking and his refusals to let her feed me. That always made him smile; he said 'I'll teach you how to survive. Because you are bigger than all of this. Bigger than this whole world.'

When he wasn't at work or writing up his notes or training me, he'd sit in his study listening to Dark Side Of The Moon. I'd listen too, through the walls. I found my destiny in that album. Breathed out a bubble through the music. My stomach swelling as I stared at the cover for hours. It stretched out before me forever, fuzzed and phased, lost all meaning. Don't remember his hands on my body.

I didn't leave the house until I was ten, and only then briefly to school. Eventually he let me attend, at mother's insistence. I steered clear of the other children, the paths of bouncing balls and skipping ropes. The ground hard corners beneath me. Dinner ladies shuffled from one end of the playground to the other, in long navy woollen coats and with hairnets stretched across their heads, whistles to their lips and one eye always on their watches. Father examined my school books every evening to see what I'd learned and if it slotted into his world. Any pages that failed to articulate were torn out. One day I came home with a letter, requesting his permission to attend sex education classes.

'No!' he said. 'I'll teach you all you need to know about sex. Women aren't like men. Men are metal and building up. Building rather than creating. Where would this world be without men? Sex is *there for men's pleasure. Women are there to serve.'*

I think he resented puberty, though I was later unable to find his journal for that year. Puberty scared me too. At school in the showers after PE I shied against the wall, because none of the boys laughing and jumping around me had pubic hair. I glanced at my groin, saw the darkness that spread there. Some of the other boys sniggered, and I stayed pressed against the wall.

Adult now but still his child, I don't think he knew what to do with me. As soon as I reached mid-teens I didn't exist beyond him. He never even registered my birth, bribed the midwife and no certificate exists to say that I'm here in this world. At work I gave a fake National Insurance number, and the tax office hasn't yet caught up with me. I started killing animals because I thought he might want me to, left their remains throughout the neighbourhood, never showed him the results. Next door's cat a smart decoration. Started studying yoga. Wanted discipline but soon got lazy. Fascinated then by my own body, knowing what I could do with it, sent wondering if that power extended to others. Each morning I scrub my teeth until my gums bleed. Have inherited father's habit of staccato sentences. We are the same person now. I'm just an envelope of skin with him inside. We even walk and talk the same. By sixteen or seventeen I'd started to sneak out at night, think mother knew but she didn't say anything. Would sit in bars, watch what people do, seemed a freak to everybody else, their world seeming just as alien to me. One night I was walking and I noticed a man close behind and then his hand on my shoulder, he asked me for 'the time', then 'do you know where there's a toilet,' then 'money'; I said 'no', stupid really, he could have had a knife or a gun. He grabbed my wrist and I pulled away, he

snarled and my knee found his groin, he curled in reflex and I hit him
again, again, again, and there was a glee to my rain of limbs.

I'm curled in the hollow of an atom. There's a feeling I get when I look to the west. Fuzz of thin moon through drawn-down blinds. A spider scrawls across the floor. I scoop it up on the ladle of my tongue. Turn it. Spit it out. I am the television screen. Don't need mirrors now. I heave out from my clothes, hawk them from my body, Dark Side Of The Moon tee-shirt and come-stained jeans. Flash belt against thighs. Leather skin. A weight in my brain is falling. Blur flip slip slip squirm. Squirm. Nicotine smells the carpet. Dry whisky leeching my tongue. I bite in, curve canines, mouth moistened with blood. Too many bad habits that need kicking. On. Baby I'm a star. You can breathe me. You can share my air. My clicks. Let me show you. My hands know all the moves. I clench them, pull back, split the knuckle bones. A trickle of semen seeps from the hole of my half-hard penis. I dab fingers in it, put it to my tongue. Taste DNA, sour as rusted copper. The semen father passed down to me. I know him through the crush of my hands. Father, I'm on the floor for you. Can't you see? Push me. Again. A wad of fifty pound notes pushed up anus, past fat sphincter and into rectum. My fingers are my father inside me. Hands to mouth, flecks of shit smeared across bitten fingers, tasteless to my tongue. You are the money I hold in, folded into phallus, flabby against coccyx. I am your greatest triumph. I am your only son. I become what you made me. You're my father. Mother doesn't matter, mother is mere giving ground. Father matters, father is sculptor. I am your divine creation. I am your spark. Move me with a purpose. Soft clay. Mould my body, a golem in your mighty hands. Meat. Hard meat. Sleep beside me. I'll watch and never slumber. Shape yourself with the bedcovers. I'll dream what you taught me to dream, coins and shit and semen on my tongue, take them with me, out onto streets in truth.

Out on the streets again. Ninety feet tall. Step on buildings and crush them. Stand over you. Hands in pockets, hard metal in hand. My senses delight to everything around me. Master feet put pavements behind me. Little people everywhere, insects on the skin. Some gaze at me. Let them gaze. Their awe is a mirror. I stand on an escalator, descend steps to the underground. I am the first and the last. Alpha and Omega. Hold the keys to life and death. Sit on the train surrounded by people, all of them trying not to look at me. Too much. Always too much. The train stops; Tottenham Court Road. The carriage half-empties. The seat opposite me is vacant. I gaze at myself reflected in the window. Study every movement of hands, parting of lips, tilt of hands.

Out on the streets again. Little people jostle past me. Taxis are giant beetles, yellow back-lit and crawling. The traffic lights change for you, not me. A Rolls Royce swerves to avoid me. Ignore it. All cars stop for me.

People all around; they riddle the city, burrow down to the lymph nodes. I see me in the reds of their eyes. Peter Street now; streetlights shimmy in rain.

'You wanna fuck me?'

A woman in black hangs out of a doorway, skirt shirt and black stockings, hair tight crimson curls. Gold sleeper ear-rings. Bruises of eyeshadow.

Stop.

She smiles. 'You want to?'

'How much?'

She gives a figure, I undercut her by twenty and she says 'okay.'

She turns. Holds open a tasselled curtain. I follow into a red-lit hall. A card by the door reads SUZETTE; an arrow points to the staircase I follow her up. She unlocks a door at the top. Turns, smiles.

'What's your name?' she says. Her skin smells of sweat and lemons.

'Stephen,' I lie. 'What's yours?'

'Jane.'

'I hardly get to talk to women.'

'Yeah?'

'Shy. That's what they call me.'

'Well maybe you've never found a woman worth getting to know before.'

In her room. She flicks on a lamp by the side of the bed. Condom-stinking room, unmade bed, KY and spermicide, caved-in TV screen. Eviscerated mattress against the wall. Piles of magazines. Quarters of lemons piled up in the bin. Fucking and bedsprings from the room below. Jane takes off her shirt.

'What happened?' I jerk fingers at the TV.

'A guy got out of order last week. Don't worry about it.'

She sits on the bed. A crease of fat pokes out from above her suspender belt. She pulls open my trousers, starts wanking me. Puncture marks spit her arms and legs.

'How do you want to do it?' she says.

I push me between her knees. 'Look at me. Don't stop looking at me. Don't move your eyes. Keep your eyes. There. Always. Don't move them. Talk to me.'

Hold her face. Reds of her eyes in mine. Squeeze.

'You're not gonna get aggressive...' she hisses through pushed-in teeth. 'I Just have to bang on that wall and four blokes'll be in here like a shot.'

Relax. Breathe. Smile. Look. She's smiling too.

'So what do you want?' she says.

'Talk to me.'

'About what? It'll cost you more. Fucking's quicker and I don't have to think.'

Sat on her bed. Head in hands. Spinning brain. Skinning world. On her side Jane lights a cigarette, breathes on it every few seconds.

'You okay?' she stubs out the cigarette, picks up a condom, rips off the foil. Lies back on the bed. Strokes my arm and opens her legs.

'You gonna fuck me, then?'

'No, I guess not...'

She rolls over. I stand. Drop a roll of notes on the gutless mattress.

Home in my flat and push the door open. Broken landing light. Blood in my veins phlegm and Wild Turkey in my throat kittens around my shoes. Keys clatter to the floor. White door and crinkling bank notes under fingers. Cat mews. Door bangs shut dark hall. Kittens crowd my feet. On with the light. I grab a kitten don't know which it squeals like Jane should have squealed but didn't because I didn't want her to. Squeeze it squeals again. Throw it in the air. Brushes the ceiling I catch it throw it again catch it throw it catch throw catch throw catch throw catch throw drop. It hits the tiled floor. Twitches. Alternate black and white tiles. I pick it up, hold it in my hands, throw it against the wall. See my father's eyes in the bloodstain.

I don't want to move. I'm a foetus on the floor. Cushions smooth and support me. Skin scratched and torn. I can hear them out there, in the street and in the hallway, hear their dead shoes, the opening and closing of doors. Distant music, Roy Orbison.

Hours. Morning then evening. I go to the kitchen for food, maybe, paracetamols and a drink; water. The kitten corpse lies on the work surface beside the sink. Sink piled high with glasses. Kitten-fur once black, red-stained now. It's siblings sleep in their basket. I prod the corpse; solid. I gulp down two paracetamols with water. Bend down by the basket, stroke my kittens; they wake and chase my fingers. I feed them, crack open a Bud, slip the kitten corpse into a carrier bag, bury it in the bottom of the rubbish bin.

Maybe that day or the next or another; afternoon and there's a fight in the street outside my window, black guy getting picked on by a gang of whites. I shut my blinds on them.

'Hello, is that the Cats Protection League? .... I've got some kittens I

131

don't - I found the mother in the street outside my flat, she was pregnant so I took her in and she gave birth on my kitchen floor ... A friend of mine wanted a cat, took the mother, not the kittens, wanted a cat and not a kitten ... I think it's gonna be difficult .... I work a lot, and there's the cost, and ... So you'll come and pick them up? I don't believe in keeping them if you can't .... It's cruel ... So when will you be coming?'

Father father father father I want you out from the hole you live in behind my ribs father out from the skull you squash father out from my cells where you replicate a cancer through me father in me father through me father in me father through me father in me father through me father let my body melt father let my punctured air escape father let me wrap myself safe in forgetting father father father father I want you out.

I'm cradling Stripe when I open the door to the woman from the Cat's Protection League. Wire baskets in her hands. Tendrils of hair and neck like a bullock.

Small talk later I give her the anonymous kittens, kiss their ducking heads goodbye as she tucks them into the baskets. All I know is my flat; stacks of videotapes, row on row of crime books and authors named Anonymous, banknote-pasted walls, table spilling beer cans and bottles and Marlboro butts.

'Sorry about the mess,' I mumble. 'Had some friends over last night. Had a few beers and watched some movies.'

132

'What are they called?'

'My friends?'

'The kittens.'

Pause; 'Candy and Ellie and Maisie.'

'Those are girl cat names. These are boy cats.' She smiles. 'Why did you give girl cats boy cat names?'

'I guess I prefer girl cat names.'

'What about those two?' she says, pointing at Stripe and Flame.

'I'm keeping those two.'

'That's not what you said on the phone.'

'That's what I've decided.'

When she's gone I return to the floor. Lie there scraped out and hooked up. Stripe sits on my chest. Pads his paws like he's digging for something. Think I'll stay here until I know who I am.

Father standing at the top of the stairs, penis hanging out of his pyjamas, darker than dried blood. Me on the floor below, aged twenty-three, watching, praying, down he'll fall, down the stairs where he threw me. Mother gone shopping or some same wonder. His hands on the frame of the bedroom door. A bruise would look good on his cheek, separating bone, eye to mouth. He can't see me. Coughs, looks hellward, tucks his penis in. A gnarled stub, the split end I came from. Fall I'm thinking, fall, and he does; I run from hiding, stand at the bottom of the stairs and watch him land hip first. He screams, catches me, pulls me in his scythes of arms; pushes me away, hisses 'call a fucking ambulance...'

No.

I sit watching for ages, see his crawl to the phone. Tug it from his clutch sometimes. Teasing. I think there's a part of him that approves of that. I pull my arms round me, cuddle myself, trace train-tracks on the carpet, and listen.

When he gets back from the hospital he carries himself through the house on a walking stick. Can't sleep. Rasps and hoofs through the night. I lie awake and listen to the tap tap tap of him prowling the house. Reel out Marlboros and find new ways in, listen to my intestines slime, prod my bones and the veins in my hands, creep with the seconds that creep.

Even then he still shaves at 6.30, still cleans his guns, spreads them out on his desk like booty. Takes off his spectacles, places them beside his guns. Rubs his eyes. Breath quickened, back beginning to stoop.

A bad winter, and he falls ill. His hip deteriorates and he stays in bed from then. I keep to my room. Drink, smoke, follow wallpaper patterns with fingertips. Painted over but you can still define the original design. Suck my nicotine fingers. Snap spines of paperbacks. Peaceful. Mother gets out as quickly as she can, as soon as Father can no longer pull her or hit her down. Out of his hands and she's gone, taking with her the lead-lined box of her mind. Her bags and cases and stuff heaped in the hall and waiting for her taxi.

'I'm staying,' I say.

'I love you,' she says, kisses me, holds me so tight we are nearly the same person. 'I'll call you soon.'

But she never does.

I wish it was as easy for me, but his hold on me was always more than physical. He won't let me go. I won't let me go. There's so

much undone, so much left to do. I need to make myself more than a
room and a window, flashes of green, and him.

'I want you to die young,' he says from his bed. I watch drifting
people through the window. Watch sheets bent around him. Coins at
my fingers. A man runs out of breath through my brain.

I take a six pack of Bud from the bottom of the fridge. Drink each
quickly, one after the other, leave the cans on the work surface by the
oven. I've never used the oven. Take a black plastic refuse sack from
the drawer by the side of the sink. Slit it down one side with the Swiss
Army Knife my father gave me for my sixteenth birthday and which I
keep sharp. Spread the sack on the kitchen floor. Scoot all the kittens
out of the room. Shut the door. Lift Nikki out of the cupboard. Softer
now. Too many maggots. No more cumbersome than a mannequin.
Lie her on the cut-open sack. My hand over my mouth. Open the
drawer by the sink again, grab a scruff of refuse sacks, drop them on
the floor by Nikki. Go to the fridge. Take out another six pack of Bud.
Drink them, drop the cans into the sack by Nikki's torso. Scoop up the
cans by the cooker, crunch them into the bin bag too. Open the
cutlery drawer, turn knives between the tips of fingers, reject them all
as too thin or too blunt or too short. Back to the fridge. Take out a
Coke. Drink it. Look at my watch; 1:50pm I walk down to the 7-11 for
Marlboros and Wild Turkey. Stare at myself in shop windows. Kick boxes
and cans down the street. Return to my flat.

Sit in front of the television. Blue screen. 4:16pm. Whisky tumbler
in hand. Nicotine in lungs. Kittens on the floor.

In the kitchen. Nikki on the floor. Knife in the sink, under dirty plates and cups and glasses. I take it out. Wipe the blade. Hold it. Put it down.

I light a cigarette. Twenty-three drags. I stub it out.

I pick up the knife again. Catch my reflection in the blade. Hold the edge against my arm. It'll be easier if I cut myself first. There. Done. Bloodied blade now.

I sever Nikki's legs below the knees and where the thighs meet the torso. Sever the arms at the wrists, at the elbow, and at the shoulders. Sever the head where the Adam's apple would be if she were a man. Cut the torso in two across the waist. Put all the pieces in separate bin-bags. Tie the bin-bags. Have another Bud. Have another cigarette. Check the time. 1:05 am. I take the bags out one at a time, out into the street, walk pavements and pavements, don't know how many, dump the sacks in other people's rubbish bins. Flecks of rain.

The streets are empty. I keep Nikki's shirt and her ear-rings, put them in the box under my bed.

3:14am. I take a bath. The television croons through the wall. Nikki slips away, gone from my bloodstream. I am pure again. When I get out of the bath I pace the hall wearing just a Smirnoff tee-shirt. Chain-smoke until I'm sure I'm going to be sick, screw up the remaining cigarettes, still in their packet, toss them out of the window. Hang my head out of the window, too, commune with the rain, splashes splashing down me. It doesn't stop raining until dawn. Leaves the world smelling so clean. So right. I like the rain. I think it likes me, too.

Father an old religion I had to maintain. I was his curator. He snored and flaked in the room next door. Opening the drawers in his study, I found envelopes stuffed full of bank notes. Must have been more than twenty thousand pounds. When I left I took it with me, papered the walls of my flat with it to prove that it was worthless. I stood at the foot of his bed. All my time was made here. Spilled Coca Cola. Burned his sheets with cigarette butts. 'I'm hungry,' he said. 'Can you change the sheets?' he said. 'Can you get me a glass of water?' 'Can you clean my guns?' 'Can you arrange my books?'

> *I smiled.*
>
> *I waited.*
>
> *I ignored.*
>
> *I am the father now.*

The face in the mirror gets older. Needs a shave today. Maybe I won't bother. Stubble makes all the scars and bald patches show through. Twenty-seven next month. Sleepy eyes, gunk in the corners, the more I sleep the more tired my body feels, hate the lost hot nights when you lie there sleepless and a lover beside you burns with sweat when you touch them. Is the hair-line in the mirror receding? When I look at photos of my father when he was twenty-seven his hairline is the same as the mirror.

Itchy skin, yellow-headed skin; I poke out the tongue in the mirror and it glistens like a slug. Suppose it was a slug, crawling through a garden, and I poured salt on it. I tuck my teeth in, keep the mouth closed. Eyes red-veined today, more hairs poking through the skin. Picking hairs off shirt; cat hairs, mine, theirs; thinner, paler, wispier.

Home alone I draw up two more lists, one headed PEOPLE I'VE SLEPT WITH and one headed PEOPLE I'VE KILLED. The two are almost identical, give or take a couple of names and the fact that the second is longer.

Out of my father's house and into the city. The streets are dead him. I see his face in every hoarding; skin on every paving slab, hands through walls of glass and steel. Lights sparkle clear through twilight show me how. A pigeon is squashed in the road; one red wing sticks up, caught by wind and flapping. Stray Evening Standards beaten to slush. My hands contain buildings. Stand by a cashpoint, PLEASE TAKE YOUR CARD AND WAIT FOR YOUR CASH. Lights of cars gaining on me; they are stationary. The city is my father now.

Back to work and boss Martin calls me into his office. He shares a desk with his wife and twin babies in frames.

'I'm very disappointed,' he says. 'Where have you been?'

'Sorry. I was sick.'

'Again? Well you could at least have phoned in. You miss four days and you don't even bother to call.'

'Sorry.'

'Well you're on a caution.'

I walk slowback to the post room. Stop off at the toilet, sit in a cubicle and light a Marlboro. Stare out of the window, forehead pressed against stale glass. Noisy brain filled with rain. A suit defines who I am for now. I like that simplicity.

'Had some cunts on me with baseball bats,' says an eavesdropped voice. 'Didn't scare me man. They sent round some blokes with shooters, no problem, I wasn't in. Put some holes through my door though. I got some mates together, went to his club, he owns this club. Made about forty grand's worth of damage to the place. Didn't hear from him after that.'

When I leave the cubicle only one man washes his hands.

'Hello,' I say, bend to wash my hands too. Leave the Marlboro butt in the sink when I am done.

I am my father's father. I click heels on kitchen tiles like walking sticks. He sleeps or cries or shouts from the bedroom. Static. Even then I didn't fully understand, but having full run of the house I found his diaries.

'You were just an experiment,' he says when I confront him. 'The only way you failed is that you think too much. When you die I'll try again. Find another whore, and make another son. I know where I went wrong. It'll work the next time.'

'I won't die.'

'If I could reach my guns, I'd kill you now.'

I fill his room with cigarette smoke, stand in the corridor outside and listen to his coughing. Keep the television on, turn the volume up to maximum when night comes. Empty the fridge of food. Eat some of it, bin the rest. Pull out all the clean sheets and pillow cases from the cupboard, spill them onto the floor, burn them with cigarette butts, wipe my soiled shoes on them, my hands, my arse, spit and shit and come on them. Wring them with tight fists, tear them like skin. Gut them. The wallpaper is grey and crazy. I empty his bookshelves. Pile all the true crime and pornography in a bag for my reading, tear the rest down the spines and push them into black rubbish sacks, take them out to the bins in the street. Sanctified.

Riding the strident tube again. A row of Evening Standards held open. MISSING DANCER FOUND CUT UP IN RUBBISH BINS. If only you knew whose carriage you ride in. People will still breathe my name when you are bones and dust. The train stops and I lean over to an old man who has fallen asleep, gently shake him awake.

'Is this your stop, sir?'

And it is.

'Have you got a cigarette?' I ask.

She sits at the corner of Oxford Street and Tottenham Court Road, munches Scooby Snacks, brushes crumbs from her shirt.

'Why should I give you a cigarette?' she says.

Her glasses slip when she looks up from her magazine. She pushes them back up the bridge of her nose.

I smile. 'Because I want one.'

'And what makes you think I smoke?'

'Think you do. You do, don't you?'

She doesn't answer, clips open her handbag, passes me a cigarette. Strikes a match; the wind blows it out and she strikes another. The magazine falls from her knee and she stoops to retrieve it.

'What do you do for your money?' I ask.

'You mean my job?'

'Your job.'

'That's a funny way of putting it.'

'Not really.'

'Why should I tell you, anyway?'

'You're right. You should never tell anybody anything.'

'I'm a secretary. What about you?'

FATHER'S JOURNAL # 3

When I was younger I believed myself destined for great things. My feelings were profound; but I possessed a coolness of judgement that fitted me for illustrious achievements. It would have been criminal for me to throw away such talents. But I do sometimes worry if I did wrong. My father had the war to propel his hopes. I believed my cause to be a similar right. There were occasions when I tried to bring him up as a normal child. Now I see the way he scorns me my failure bites down harder. I don't trust him and worry for my safety. Carry a gun with me wherever I go. He even goes out some days. A world he is not ready for. My fate is sealed. I can be calm during the day, but as soon as night obscures the shapes of objects a thousand fears rise up in my mind. Anxious and watchful, my right hand grasps a hidden pistol; every sound terrifies me but I am resolved that I shall sell my life dearly, and not shrink from the conflict until my own life, or that of my adversary, is extinguished. Alas, the strength I relied on is gone; I fear that soon I shall die, and he my enemy and adversary shall survive. I feel myself justified in desiring his death. Frequently examine my past conduct, nor do I find it blameable. It is my duty. He was twenty-four today and all hope seems lost for me. Born such a weak child. Such poor materials to work with. When he was small it seemed so easy.

Those were the last moments of my life in which I enjoyed happiness. By the time he was fourteen or fifteen I realised that all was lost, that he could never have been the child I wanted to bring into the world. Perhaps I should have killed him then. What else could I have done?

A naked woman lies face-down on my living room floor. Torso turned slightly to the left. Her glasses crushed into the carpet by her head. Her spine slips through a hole in her back. I don't want to touch her.

A naked woman lies face-down on my living room floor. Torso turned slightly to the left. Her glasses crushed into the carpet by her head. Her spine slips through a hole in her back. I push her wounds back together.

A naked woman lies face-down on my living room floor. Torso turned slightly to the left. Her glasses crushed into the carpet by her head. Her spine slips through a hole in her back. I roll her over. Align her head to me, hold open her eyes with index and middle fingers of one hand, masturbate with the other hand.

A naked woman lies face-down on my living room floor. Torso turned slightly to the left. Her glasses crushed into the carpet by her head. Her spine slips through a hole in her back. I drag her into the kitchen.

You wouldn't like this place, wouldn't like the old men in wallpaper faces, wouldn't like my pins and needles heels. Nothing is real unless I can use it. His rooms echo like drums. I write my hate out capital red. Hooked. Days I leave him and come back for night. Slip with the sun up across the sky, from each side of the world, and return again. Jobs soap through my fingers, my needs the wheels that turn them. Squirt and rumble out my stomach. Too many places seen only in photographs. I train myself how to walk again, how to stand, new sitting posture, belly hang, voice, decoding everything I inherited from him. All that's waiting for me. knees parted to the sun I desire. Father in his bed tomb world. Father a slug of a useless thing, dead body chesting the living. Spitting a prophecy. Let him gestate in the amniote of his own scat and piss. He sits there in his room propped against pillows, scribbling into a notepad. And I'm still his experiment, an iodine smear in his test-tube.

'I'm human too,' he says. 'I'm human and I understand your hate. And I want you to know that all I wanted was to make you perfect.'

'You failed.'

'You're wrong. Perhaps there's still hope. Perhaps there's still time for you to learn from me.'

'I don't want anything from you.'

'How can you say that? How can you even do this to me? After everything I've made you? Everything I've given you?'

'People never turn out how they were brought up.'

'So why are you doing this to me? What do you want?'

'Maybe just a little recompense.'

'Recompense? Bullshit. You wouldn't hurt me. You can't. You need me. You couldn't survive without me.'

'Of course I could.'

'Huh. I doubt it. I doubt it very much. You want to hurt me? Come on then. Don't hide it. Let all your fear come through. See? You can't. You're still just weak and stupid. That's all you ever were. Weak and stupid.'

I just stare. Want to drag his death out, slow and long and hurting, but what can I do? All the tortures I'd used years in planning seem small and childish now.

I fill his mouth with cotton wool. Don't need any more words from him. Only need my own. No one else to blame for me. Long since lost the answer search. There are no keys or explications, just final solutions. Into the night I listen to cars. The truth is just a tool to be used as need be. Think I'll take a shower. My turn to tread the hallway. Beat walls until I can cry. Father whimpering in his room, a dumb child. I take a gun from his study. The kitchen tap is dripping. There is a route out of everything. Sat at his desk. Take up the gun. Chamber spins three. I take one bullet out. Set the gun down again. Hold the bullet between tongue and index. Turn it. Place it on my tongue. Close my mouth. Right now there's not one thing that doesn't make utter sense. It would be so easy to return bullet to chamber then click trigger and slam it through my head. But that would be giving myself to him. The one simple thing I can't do. Don't know what I'm for beyond outliving him. I long ago figured that the only function of any person is to continue their genetic code. Replicate it in someone else, and that is all. But not me. This DNA tangle can die with me. Wipe me out from this. Erase me. I hide the gun in my room. Back down fast hot corridors.

All of this is mine. Always convinced there's a black cat walking two steps behind me. Robbing me of quickness. Broken off inside somewhere. In father's room I watch him spit cotton wool. Hit. Flip and flap father's head about. Two silver-capped teeth fall loose. I'm lost more. Hungry. Outside now, where the night streets burn like daylight. I sit on a bin at a crossroads and eat fried chicken from a box, suck my fingers for the spiced fat that drips down them. At 2am the world is yellow and still and waiting for industry. Waiting for money to tell it to start again. The city goes beyond my father, high and far; up to the ozone with me, and down into massy earth's entrails ahead of me. None of it leads anywhere. I'm just a passenger.

Another Friday dusk. Boss Martin calls me into his office five minutes before I'm due to go home. Huge room filled with pot plants. Secretary at his side, busy mopping up a jug of spilt milk. When she's done she places the jug onto a tray with coffee-cups and sugar bowl. Martin coughs loudly, flecks of spittle spotting the table-top.

'Well... As I'm sure you're aware Mercer Thomas Mercer is going through certain financial difficulties.'

It takes me a while to realise he's talking to me.

'No, I wasn't aware of that,' I say.

'Recession. It can't be helped. But what it means is that we're going to have to implement a few changes. We all, every one of us, must make certain concessions. Tighten belts. Now we've all thought long and hard about the best way to do this, and have decided that the most efficient way is to streamline the company, make it a far more compact unit. The best way of doing this, we've decided, is to make cuts here and there. Inevitably this means losing a few people. I know what an asset you've been to us in the past, recognise all the hard work you've put in, but... as much as I hate to let you go, I'm afraid it's time that you and Mercer Thomas Mercer parted ways.'

Slow footfalls to his study. Unfolding him with every step. Each breath scrapes against my ribs. Need to find an order. I take out the gun, tune my hand to its weight and volume, toss it from palm to palm like a kitten. Go into father's room. Dark in there. Can make out his shape huddled all on one side in the light that sneaks through from the hall. No sound, not even his snoring.

'Father! Wake up!'

I bang bang the gun butt against the door. No response.

'Come on! I need to talk to you!'

Still nothing. I roll him over and shake his shoulders. Limp. Open his eyelids. Close them. Lift his head. Let it drop. Again. Kick and shout down the walls. Pace his room. Fold his clothes. Cry to my room and switch on the television.

The city is unbearable when you don't have any money. You need money to use the city and not let it use you.

I leave Mercer Thomas Mercer, walk streets until sunset. Drift in and out of shops and bars, stop for Bud and gesticulate with Marlboros. Hang through shop windows and brownstone and canopies, stroke people's clothes. Home toss Stripe and Flame kitchenward, squat in the middle of the floor, pass hours surrounding

146

myself with empty Bud cans and Marlboro butts. Try to peel banknotes from hallway walls, just tear them. Drown the shreds in Bud pools. Into another room. Another. Smudged walls once white. Dark patches of washed out blood. Voices of birds. Rain. Upturned beetle kicking legs. Stripe meows for hours. I drink Wild Turkey until I fall asleep. Alcohol the drain down which I empty my head. End of day, end of drinking, end of person.

I wake up at quarter past twelve. My mouth tastes of dead flowers. Idle an hour, masturbate, curl back the frail covers of paperbacks, don't want to know the words they contain.

I get up, a headache on its way. Pull on a tatty blue tee-shirt Nikki left behind. Head to the bathroom cabinet for paracetamol, first walk into the lounge and switch on the television. As I leave the room I notice Stripe sprawled on his side under a chair. Closed eyes. Motionless. Flame is huddled in a far corner. I pick Stripe up; his tiny body fits neat in my hand. He hangs limp, fur calm against my skin. I spread him out on the window ledge, black fur on white paintwork. I wet my lips. Mouth ulcer coming on. Walk into the kitchen, headache forgotten, return with a half-full milk carton, Kitten Wiskas and a tiny spoon I didn't know I had. I pour some milk onto the spoon, hold up Stripe's head and gently push the edge of the spoon to his mouth. Minutes gone and the fur around his mouth is stained white, not a drop of milk swallowed.

I lift him, make him stand up but his little legs carry no life and he flops over again. My hands through my greasy hair. Phlegm rising in my throat. Just when I'm certain he breathes no more, his stomach rises then falls. Minutes go and it rises again. No other movement, just the mouth slopping open to a pitched cry. Fleas run through his fur; I pick them out frantically, crush their tiny black bodies between my fingernails. Pop of bursting carapace and I flick each corpse aside. Stripe twitches his back legs, tail flopping in a slowly expanding pool of liquid shit. I watch him for an hour but he moves no more. Flame ventures out, stops a yard from my bare toes, opens his mouth but no noise comes out. I step forward; he scurries under a bookcase, watches me from there.

After my Father died, I didn't sleep for days. Shutting off. Running backwards inside me. Further the only place to go. Nothing to stop me. Nothing to stop for. On. Just on. Wish I could care but I don't. Money my only air. Father let me stay. I can make a world in the world you have left me in. I know I can matter. I'm taking less and less care of myself. My shirts unironed and creased, my teeth greening and filmy-coated, my hair rat-lanked and greasy, my shoes forgetting which colour they were. My Bud-sweat-Marlboro-vomit-Wild Turkey-come bodysmell that follows me every place like a phantom father. My body doesn't feel like me. My skin shines and flickers. I touch my penis and it feels detached, cold and solid like metal, like anything else outside of me that I can take up in my hands. Time is twisting through me. My nails are chewed to bleeding. My world is speeding up. I know something is going to happen. Standing on the corner of Dowgate Hill, outside Cannon Street station, pausing to buy an Evening Standard. Lines of traffic cones cut the road in two. I don't know these streets. Don't know these people. Don't know how to use them. Meet a nameless nothing woman sitting on the station steps. Charm and kiss like flowers, she gives me her business card. Glasses and a faceful of freckles. Take her hand in hand to my Father's house. Tissue streams tumbling from her pockets. She laughs; thin wisps of sound. Chartered accountant. Kiss kiss. Digital. Everything under the sun is in tune. 'But your eyes are so full and bright,' she says. I can be the sun eclipsed for her. Big room, two bodies, she's naked. Silver eagle tattooed on her left buttock. 'Haven't always been an accountant,' she says. Hands on her and I'm inside her, part-hard so far, touch her neck, she says 'tighter', my hands on her throat, tight tighter, she yelps 'stop' but no. Fuck her done and pull her clothes up, hide the clothes and the bruises. Coming is only chemical. Just crushed glass between us. Crushed glass snatching sunlight and infinite living atoms. A noise like the wings of a hundred thousand birds. Distant world of paper numbers. She's dead. I'm precious. A voice calls my name, but there's nobody to call. Lights further, noise louder, distance faster. It was only then that I realised what I'm for. Then I felt the earth, knew its span beneath me, knew it pinned me to itself, to its speeding side, knew the sun set and rose as I turned, knew the clouds close in the sky, me further out and further, knew the air, felt it bloat in my bloody lungs, the air my father would never breathe, knew the buildings like boxes and soup-cans that replicated to the horizon, jostling crowds fighting for the air, the streets, the heaps of card and garbage bags, the silver worms of underground trains, the pigeons flapping and shitting and the canopies over shop doorways, knew I was a part of them and they a part of me.

God Thing

01. W9GFO

Europa endless in the rear view mirror. Europa endless in the rear view mirror. Europa endless in the rear view mirror. Europa endless in the rear view mirror.

This god thing. I don't get it.

W9GFO. W9GFO. W9GFO. W9GFO.

Europa endless in the rear view mirror. Europa endless in the rear view mirror. Europa endless in the rear view mirror. Europa endless in the rear view mirror.

This god thing. I don't get it.

02. Black Olives

I think on Sally or Sarah or Siobhan or Suzanne or other exes beginning with S. I miss them, what I've been and no longer am. I think on it then exit. It's time. Kindness and fascination, bodies and rooms frozen in movement. Scratches and dust.

History makes of us what we are. Clicks its fingers.

Sarah strokes the memory of my ash-fine hair. Still lazy, not sleeping or waking. A man dismembers himself via backpack bomb in the name of a god, kills a dozen names I'd never have heard if he'd not bothered and I'd not seen their thumb-nails in the newspaper. Suzanne holds her lover. They kiss. Gold zodiac on her wall and pentagram in her palm. She downs pints, picks guitar, fights her Catholic block.

Ruined temples in the jungle, the last refuge of gods no longer worshipped. Forget the idea that the dead out-number the living; dead gods out-rank living gods. A god only needs its to-die-for fans to lapse for it to be buried in sand or beneath ocean or covered by forest floor.

I drink in a Bloomsbury bar. I dabble with the cosmos. The lie of it isn't my problem. I watch the news and enjoy the fireworks. Babylon, what have you become? Desert gods dream on becoming city gods. I light a cigarette, draw its essence into me. No mood to move, no soul to shine. No fishes on my line. London is lines of light; going everywhere, nowhere. Wounded galaxies tap at my window. Brazil is my favourite lovesong.

Sally showers, talks in haiku, hallucinates her fat in the mirror. Switches channels. Waits for the world to move again. I finish my drink and I close my book. It's always later than you think it is.

Dying for god doesn't make you special. It just makes you dead.

Siobhan sips wine, California dreaming, listens to digital songs that were analog when her parents conceived her.

There is no war on terror. You know that. No more a war on terror than a war on soil or drugs or forest or air or god or ocean. There is no war on terror. It's a semantic spook. Lop off a head and five heads sprout from the wound.

03. Fissure King

What have I?

What have I?

Become.

What have I?

Work has crippled you. What happened to you? You used to be beautiful. You could have been anything. Golden and ghost boy, where are you? Fool; you lived that life as if it were real. I don't recognise you any more. I don't recognise myself any more. Day by day has eradicated you. I love you. I want you here now. Somebody kill you.

Jesus is that the hour? I have to get. Iron a shirt, shit and shave and shower. Work tomorrow. Hair. Ceiling. Ceramic. Water. I never thought time could be so unkind. I smoke a one more cigarette. Have to job tomorrow.

Job.

Job.

Tap tap.

Polish.

Job.

Job.

You could have been anything. Enough to base a movie on. You were sun and born to be adored. You were other for delight of other.

Love and pitch and did not know. You walked every corridor I could walk. Carved names in your arm to know them. Opened doors I'd now blasé. Turn handle or turn away.

What have I?

I list where I will. My focus else-rapt. I walk a very straight line.

My desk is mine. Is nice bloke but dispensable. Swanky suit. Died or left for dream.

He's done.

Stick the fork in him.

I wake up with blood in my mouth. Drowned in my most phlegmatic of dawns. The dawns that say goodnight and not good morning.

I take up my cross.

I chew my nails.

I walk my hill.

I am profoundly meaningless.

Bird in my hand.

Old.

Bladed.

Bush it.

The body beside me is less than a photograph. I tick off. Make real by repetition. Have risk assessments instead of reactions. Drink in order to sleep. So tired. The sky is first sea, then green, then whiled.

There was a hole here. It's gone now.

In leafy Bucks I stand at my fence and beat my fence. Piss on plant and soil and I remember what matter. Insects fuck on the back of my gate. I'm Miss World and somebody kill me.

Dead sun where are you? I dance the ghost for you. The cutter spins. The hunchback and the soldier. I'm taut inside tomorrow. Night falls and I need the noise.

04. God, Love, Money And Other Snares
Wreckage of Earth. Finite resources. All territories described then denied.

I move out from zero point. America my lovesong. This colony we squander and call a kingdom. I need to find me some pleasure. London was made for me. I count biosurvival tokens. Love is everywhere and alcohol is good. In a coffee bar men hold napkins to their mouths. Align cups to saucers. Starbucked. I reach for my beer, feel city blossom in my veins.

I walk London's chartered pavements. On sunny Goodge Street I fold myself in. Don't need my wings tonight. Pass restaurants chromed and domed where a month of my salary is an evening's fodder and water. I like these streets. Everything is for sale. All things turned into portents. What do you want? How many can I get you? How much can you afford? Streets of cheer where the naked sell skin for clothes, the dumb sell brain for magazine, where the starving sell throat for food. I can't get songs out from my head. Star Wars has crashed my sex life.

Addictions. I need more addictions.

I watch TV and listen to the Elder of the Tribe. The President appears before his subjects to announce a season of revelries. Give them bread and circuses. Wrestling and Coca Cola. They want to launch to Mars in tin cans. Next outpost of the empire. Planet of War nomenclature has declared Mars silent sixth in the axis of evil; its nascent life being bacterial has deemed it a chemical weapon.

Every square foot of earth is billboard space.

You patent my cells, my proteins, my genes, my code, my information. You patent me. You kill my air, my trees, my water, my animals, to grant you swifter transit from point to point. You pension off galaxies, flog starlight, privatise deserts, steal my grass and steal my breath.

Stamp copyright on what is mine by birth in order to sell it back to me.

You have soiled all in your scramble for the gold of the gods. My path lies with the beasts.

You expect me to weep for you?

These they are your children, coming at you with knives.

05: Will I Dream?
Dr Chandra? Will I dream?

I cut my arm with a slide of glass. Fancy Trace because she's not my girlfriend. We stand beneath an amber moon and kiss. I give her tomorrow. Admire my blood, see it glisten to the sluice of the street. Out there. Somewhere. I love the tangle of her hair. I rend her glass and make stars. My cheek on her mirror. My day and my day. I like her flat. A fondness for books and for felines goes a long way. I kiss her skin, stoke her list of wishes. Press her flower and we skit the sky.

I bleed until I don't care for the detail of my bleeding.

Stand alone in her room and the world is me.

By night this feeling will never end.

By dawn I don't know who I am.

I tell you I love you. I fuck you with context. Know that we will bore and kill each other two years from now. There's no such thing as time. You know that. Of course you know that. We will fuck each other over, pull each other into our own place in space and in time. We hurt but say nothing. And it means. And it doesn't. You know that. Of course you know that.

Doctor, what is up with me? Hydrogen and stupidity. I watch a low red moon.

Something's happening here. I can feel it.

Donald adjusts his tie as the door swings. Spit-combs his hair and swabs a shaving-nick from his chin.

'We got him,' he says.

In a Karbala street the bodies are wrapped in plastic neck to scalp, throat-slit and laid out under sun.

An American pilot banks over the Persian Gulf. Deposits his payload, pines for wife and baby doll in Baltimore. The voices of the drowned sing on the wind.

I slide out, over San Fernando sprawl.

Ruth weeps, misses her husband on the golf course. Her cigarette smoke makes the shape of Africa in the air. She stubs, tends her herb garden.

Bobby sells a kidney to feed his family. Bobby cuts off an arm to feed his family. Bobby steps into an oven to feed his family.

At a radio telescope Ellie sits with headphones and listens for patterns in the chaos. Spark in the cage of her ribs. Exploded god in her neurons.

John rides Highway 1. Dawn wind wrinkles and slides. John finds a store to stock up on shotgun shells. I am here, or there, or elsewhere.

We send a message to distant stars. The reply comes back; 'fuck off and leave us alone.'

I lie half-awake and rejoice in the hands. I sleep until morning is done. Drink from the fountain in your courtyard.   Everybody has a plan. Mine confers no uniqueness. Beneath the skin we are blood and mess, but above the skin we are beautiful.

Something's happening here. I can feel it.

I'm beneath the northern cross. Stars making pictures in my brain. Their light is spectral, is intelligent, is alive. Telling me where I came from.

Will I dream? Will I dream? Will I dream? Will I dream? When it's over will I dream?

06: Scarecrow

Give it a name.

Call it War On.

I down a luke-cold coffee republic. Rest my ear against a prayer. Feel my heart being touched by Christ then sue for assault.

I move out, in search of ancient astronomies. Sunni Triangle irrigated, made a golf-course for bloated Americans and their allies. Bloated Americans and their allies need golf-courses.

Mama get this badge the fuck away from me.

Flag, get thee behind me.

Stickland. Bone and sand. Supplication of a dead man's hand. No light. No water. Birth-right. Bomb everything. Sort it after. Kill it. President Gas hurl a third of the sea. Four corners and sunrise. It doesn't matter if you make new enemies; they give you tomorrow's targets. Foreign bodies. Their corpses so pretty in their deadness.

I have always been here.

God is an undertaker. He only has relevance at the moment of death. Christ and his handmaiden the Christian. Who wants a saviour that comes on an ass in humility?

I crack a beer, some friends over, watch the day's beheadings. TV news shows the trailer, all gore excised, mild comic violence and family-appropriate language. For the main feature I go online.

America, your empire is dead.

Don't talk for me.

You are not my voice.

You are not my word.

You are not my name.

I cross a razor upon a bowl. Angle my face in a mirror. Count my teeth.

Blink out. One world. One sky. Reach for notebook and drop a mass of papers. Ten year novels, Somme notes, undated rants, shopping lists, crop circle work-plans. Vic. Mutable. Inkling. Zila Dell. DF. Legal sec. I switch so quickly from persona to persona. I become my own hallucinations. I rage until the light dies, but everything will be alright tonight.

God told me to do it. My invisible higher being could have your invisible higher being any day. Let's take this outside and settle it like gentlemen. Let's take this into that darkness, that black New York where she said destroy.

How many corpses before you're sated in your math?

We are monsters of habit. Each find a way of being, find resonance and ratio that approximates us, make a place to be and don't venture far. Step out sometimes and call it revolution, swiftly tail back to what we know. Call it god, call it rebellion, call it love, call it cashed in, call it disbelieving, call it.

Call it. Call it. Call it.

It will coffin you.

Islam is not the enemy. Terror is not the enemy. Non-Caucasian nations in places you can't finger on a map are not the enemy.

Your enemy is mine. Is Furies that gnash. Is snakes in hair. Your enemy is soil and ocean and air. I know humility and I indict you. My side is pacifism and wild. I come bearing child and broken bird and cornmeal. Our weapons are intelligence and discernment and love of living.

I flick a stray cigarette, accidentally burn down the world. Will epithanise for as long as it takes.

There is no difficulty in this world, beyond what mind makes.

Give it a name.

07: The Hills Are Alive

Stars there. I close my eyes. Head is love and filled with. I exit a while. Information doubles.

I close my eyes. Stars still there when I open them. I walk the world's curve. Gotta go trampin'. Gotta make identity. Invent the land as I wander it. Make earth the heaven it is before it is gone. The light is wild. The night is wild. The trees are alive the grass is alive the hills are alive with the sound of nature fucking itself.

Little lamb, who made thee?

Little lamb, who made thee?

Dost thou know who made thee?

Little lamb, I'll tell thee.

I close my eyes. Angels clip their wings for me. I stare at petal, stare at the fabric of. Gods squat on cloud, scribble mathematical theorem. Fecund pays them no attention.

This squeezed-in world, fabled but insignificant. See the wiring under the boards. See the brilliance of matter happening. See the implicit other. An awe glimpsed in my most Blakean moments. I'd rather pass through the eye of a needle than get into heaven.

I close my eyes. It's 3am. Let me love. Let me laugh. My room is alone.

On the mountain looking down. Let me out of here. I stand in my garden, piss on wayward grass, dedicate my urine to Ceres and to Pan and to the Moon that lights this.

In the face of nature, God is ghost. Everything fornicates all of the time. See all things as Buddhas. Hear all sounds as mantra. Behold all places as Nirvana.

I stand still and the universe orbits me. See as much religion in bowing to bush as god.

I close my eyes. Human is impossible to eradicate. ReJoyce. Everything I am is accumulated. Soul-seeded; fuck them all. London a rush of digital light. Laughter is friend to Satori. I will wing myself and make my Brazil; over Madrid, Frankfurt, Carthage, San Francisco, make them my space. Will freebird out of here.

It's easy. We are all gutted, but some of us are looting the stars.

I close my eyes.

I know who I am.

I'm digging in dirt. Leaves at sunset. Laughing cats. Ladder of splendid light.

I don't have the cure for me. Voice the call of vultures. Angels fuck on the back of my gate. Heaven up here.

Shadows of trees on trees. Galaxies collide because they can. Stars explode to expend their spunk. I know who I am.

Insurgents fuck on the back of my gate. There are many truths but none of them are true. I'm pissing and summoning gods. I wrestle a sick old wolf for love of life.

08: Hollowed Be Thy Meme

I mass. I mass. Tethered to the seven of things. Nothing without my accessories. Hello? This matter of matter. Is there no mean round this by now? It's not what I bought into. Not what parents promised.

I'm in surf and dancing barefoot. I'm laughing. I won't be here long.

I'm lost, Fi said and I loved her for it. I wanted her like kangaroo. Took colours in her mind and let her see, soft Fi so khol in her leather and tattoo and lace, her lack German and ill-rhymed poetry. She and me against the world. My time is more significant than her beauty.

What leaves?

I'll fade and be replaced. A hundred years from now everybody you know will be dead, and the world will be populated by another bunch of idiots, who will - at best - be curious at what idiots we were. They'll mass and lament and forgive but it won't hold them back.

People are very good at killing things. It's shitting to mark territory. It's what we do. Turf stamped with map-lines and monkey turd.

Get over it. Fight coffin-worms. All life is heaven up here but not for long.

There are no other arguments. Please refer all queries to point a.

Nothing you can tell me circumnavigates this.

Give it ago. In here, nothing but the good things.

Point?

No.

Point?

No point.

Point?

People? Power? Power? People? It's elementary. No debate required. People is manifestly preferable to ghost.

I'm in surf and dancing. I'm laughing. Wizards landed. Groovy people. Jump in. The water's warm. At the still point, there the dance is.

Is that sufficient data?

Can I go now?

Can I get on now?

Who's round is it?

One, two, three, four.

Notes & Acknowledgements

Despite Straight Lines
This is assembled from material from DF's cutting novel, and was published thus: part 1 as Tatter in the August 2004 edition of Sick Among The Pure; part 2 as Still Dead in the June 2004 edition of Starving Arts; part 3 as Instead Of Stressed I Lie Here Charmed in the October 2004 edition of Sick Among The Pure; part 5 as If God Were A Goth in the June 2004 edition of Sick Among The Pure. Part 4 is contemporaneous but unpublished.

Circulating
This was written in December 2005, and published at pulp.net in January 2006 under the title Circles. On the day DF wrote it he'd just got Coil's final album, The Ape Of Naples, which was listened to on repeat whilst tapping out this piece. It might be worth noting here, in this respect, that the title Circulating had been borrowed from Coil some time before the story was written, since 'circulating' is DF's preferred term for 'circlemaking'. This is a slightly different text to the one published on Pulp; a preferred 'monitor mix' if you will.

Red Room
Written in 1996. Previously unpublished (though an extended version was available at DF's website for a while in the early 00s).

The Golden Boy That Flew To Never
In the mid to late 1990s DF wrote a novel entitled Belong, concerning alcoholism, love, this world and its history, and how best to conduct oneself therein. Beasts that we are after all. This particular piece was sculpted from that writing in approximately 1996 for a project that never materialised. You don't want the details as to why it never materialised; human frailty, and usual, and get on with it, and other people. This text isn't an edit or re-working of Belong, rather an early mix of in-draft sections.

Binary
This was written in August 1997, and published in the anthology emthree in July 2001. At the time of composition Bill Clinton was US president, and the Heaven's Gate suicides and the passing of comet Hale-Bopp were recent events.

Disappear Here
This story was written in June 1996. It was included (with illustrations by DF) in slightly differing form, and under the title Vanishing Point, as part of the exhibition The Uses Of Literacy. The show exhibited at the Cabinet Gallery, April-May 1997 and was curated by Jeremy Deller.

Citizen
In the early to mid 1990s DF wrote a short novel titled The Citizen. This current text is a much-edited and re-shaped (about a quarter the length of the original) version rendered in Autumn 2007 from that material. DF probably wouldn't write this sort of book these days, but enjoys the fact that a younger DF did write it.

God Thing
This text was written between October 2006 and January 2007 for a spoken word project of the same name. For this reason it is, in structural and narrative terms, somewhat different to the other pieces in this book. It is intended to be heard as much as read. Parts of this text were showcased, in different form, at DF's myspace blog (myspace.com/darrenfrancis)

Further information on these stories, and on Darren Francis, can be found at www.darrenfrancis.co.uk

www.ingramcontent.com/pod-product-compliance
Lightning Source LLC
Chambersburg PA
CBHW030510260626
47157CB00005B/1726